Suffer Little Children

Suffer Little Children

Thomas D. Davis

Walker and Company
New York

First published in the United States of America in 1991
by Walker Publishing Company, Inc.
Published simultaneously in Canada by Thomas Allen & Son
Canada, Limited, Markham, Ontario

Library of Congress Cataloging-in-Publication Data
Davis, Thomas D., 1941-
Suffer little children / Thomas D. Davis.
p.   cm.
ISBN 0-8027-3205-4
I. Title.
PS3554.A937774S84   1991
813'.54--dc20   91-29975
CIP

Grateful acknowledgment is made for permission to reprint lyrics from the
following: "Today I Started Loving You Again" [p. 54], by Merle Haggard &
Bonnie Owens. Copyright © 1968 & 1969 Tree Publishing Co., Inc. (All
rights administered by Sony Music Publishing, 8 Music Square, West,
Nashville, TN 37203); and "Just in Case a Night Like This One Never
Comes Again" [p. 155], by Tom Davis, © 1972 Temi Combine Inc.
(All rights controlled by Combine Music Corp. and administered
by EMI Blackwood Music Inc.).

Printed in the United States of America
2 4 6 8 10 9 7 5 3 1

To Diane, with love

I am a bug, and I recognize in all humility
that I cannot understand why the world is
arranged as it is. Men are themselves to
blame, I suppose; they were given paradise,
they wanted freedom, and stole fire from
heaven, though they knew they would become
unhappy, so there is no need to pity them. . . .
But then there are the children, and
what am I to do about them?

Dostoyevski, *The Brothers Karamazov*

Chapter 1

THE BABY WAS BAPTIZED one Sunday in May. We were in a church full of flowers, the baby lying in Katie's arms, a children's choir singing "Jesus Loves Me."

We came home, had Sunday dinner, put the baby down, then lay down ourselves, making love as an excuse to be close. I fell asleep holding Katie, then woke hearing her scream. She was across the room, staring down at our crib-dead child.

Katie's scream never really stopped. She held on to her grief as if it were a second child she was determined never to lose. No one could take it from her—not me, not her friends, not the doctors who treated her after her first suicide attempt.

She got what she wanted, finally, on another Sunday, lying in a hot bath with her wrists slashed. I thought by then I'd mourned her already, but I was wrong. That first night alone I cried until I vomited, then stumbled outside into the darkness, trying to breathe. I ended up on my back in the grass, staring into the heavens of the God who'd let my wife and baby die. I said: Tell me again how great Thou art, you bastard.

I don't go into churches much anymore.

$\triangledown$

Chapter 2

Bʊᴛ ᴛʜɪs ᴡᴀs ʙᴜsɪɴᴇss.

I entered the sanctuary and looked around. The air felt cool and sterile. The altar and the empty wooden pews had the highly polished sheen of precious unused things. There were stained-glass windows portraying saints who seemed content and lifeless. The room was like an abstraction, a place without human frailty or suffering.

But the solitary man in the front row was real enough, and he seemed to have all the suffering he could handle. He was not so much bent forward as doubled over. His muttered prayers sounded like groans.

He didn't hear me approach. He was a thick-shouldered man with a full head of white hair. The hands he held out in prayer twisted together like two angry wrestlers.

I spoke softly, trying not to startle him. "Reverend Bauer."

He must have misjudged the direction of the voice because he glanced up toward the altar. Above the altar was a large stained-glass window that showed a seated Jesus, mild as a middle-aged baby-sitter, surrounded by children who tugged at the hem of his robe. The inscription at the base of the window said, "Suffer little children to come unto me. Luke 18:16."

I spoke again, and Bauer noticed me. He didn't sit up or turn.

"What?" he said, in a voice thick with exhaustion.

"I'm sorry to intrude. Your secretary said I should look for you here. I'm Dave Strickland. Frank Edmundson sent me."

"You're the detective?"

"Yes."

"I don't want you here."

"You want to talk later?"

"I don't want to talk at all. I don't want your help."

Bauer was hunched forward, staring at the floor. His hands gripped folds of material at the thighs of his black suit pants, as if he was keeping himself from tumbling over.

"Frank said you were reluctant at first. But he said you'd agreed."

"I've changed my mind." Bauer was speaking with difficulty, like a man out of breath. "I'm sorry you came all this way for nothing. But I don't want your help. Please go."

"Couldn't we talk about it for a few minutes?" I asked. When he didn't respond, I tried again. "Reverend Bauer . . ."

"Please . . . leave me alone."

Bauer stood and turned, and the look of him surprised me. The smooth white hair had suggested slick images of television evangelists I had passed, as quickly as possible, on my way to other channels. But Bauer had a roughed-up working man's face. A drinking man's face too, judging from the broken capillaries in his nose and cheeks. His eyes were painfully bloodshot.

"I'll go," I said. "But I'd like an explanation first."

"I don't have to explain myself to you."

"No, you don't. But I have come a long way."

"I know. I'm sorry. Frank will pay you for your trouble, won't he? If not, I guess I could . . ."

"Never mind. The money's all taken care of. I'd just like to know why you don't want my help."

"It's nothing against you. If you'd been here that first night . . ." Bauer's eyes seemed to shift from me to some distant place. "I felt so desperate. I was running everywhere, begging people's help. The police, the neighbors, the congregation—they all did what they could. But there was so much else that could have been done. I was frantic, I thought I was coming apart. Then suddenly I seemed to hear the words of our Lord: 'Why are ye so fearful? How is it that ye have no faith?' "

Bauer's eyes came back to me. My face must not have shown the reaction he wanted, for he said: "Are you a Christian?"

"No."

"Then you can't understand. We believe in a God who can do anything. A God who loves us, who listens to our prayers. He asks us to trust in Him. Am I really trusting in Him if I run around seeking help from the world like a desperate unbeliever?"

"I thought God helps those who help themselves."

Bauer frowned. "I think you're speaking as a cynic."

"Maybe I am. But you're speaking like a Christian Science parent who wants to deny medical help to a child. You don't believe that sort of thing, do you? You don't believe that Christians should do nothing."

"I don't believe in the Christian Science philosophy. But I do believe we Christians have too little faith in God. Martha and I were reading a book on the power of prayer last month, and I believe now that it was a sign from God. The book chastises Christians for expecting too little of God. It asks how we can believe in the God we do and not expect miracles. The lack of miracles these days isn't God's doing; it's ours. It's our lack of faith. The book talks of Jacob and the angel of God. When the angel denied him, Jacob didn't come running back with one of those cute little stories we tell our Sunday-school children about how God answers prayers by saying no. Jacob wrestled with the angel. Even when the angel hurt him, Jacob hung on. He said: 'I will not let thee go except thou bless me.' And Jacob prevailed."

Bauer's voice was filled with passion, with a determination to convince. But I had a feeling it wasn't me he was trying to convince. As his words died away in the empty church, I said: "You're right: I can't understand. If a child of mine were missing, nothing would keep me from doing everything I could to find him."

"But then, you're not a believer."

"I believe, God's on the side with the biggest guns."

Bauer's face made an instant shift from religious passion to righteous anger, like one of those trick drawings that can be seen as two different things. He said: "That's blasphemy. And this is the Lord's house."

"Reverend, it's just another building to me."

"Then get out of it."

"I will."

But Bauer wouldn't leave it at that. "I pity you. It must be terrible to live without God."

"Yeah, well, I pity us all. Mostly I pity your son. I'm sure he'd be comforted to know that he's being used as a test case for your faith."

"How dare you!"

Bauer took a couple of steps toward me with his fists clenched. What I was seeing now didn't look like righteous anger. It looked like the moves of a bar fighter. I didn't want to tangle with this large man crazed with grief and faith and maybe alcohol. And I didn't feel so good about having pushed him. He had troubles enough.

"Take it easy," I said, holding up my palms. "I'm going. I'm sorry about your son. I really am. I hope he'll be all right."

I turned and started up the aisle. I could feel depression coming on like a hangover from that pointless confrontation.

"Wait!"

The word sounded like a cry of pain. I turned back. Bauer hadn't moved.

"If I had faith enough, I wouldn't need you," he said. He made it sound like an accusation against me.

"Maybe you just love your son."

"I do love him," said Bauer fiercely. "It's not that I don't trust the Lord. It's that I don't trust myself. I'm not sure I have faith enough, and I don't want Billy to pay for my failings. And this may be a punishment on me for . . ." He left off speaking, but the way his face worked I had the feeling he was finishing the confession in his head. After a moment, he said: "Please help us."

"There are no guarantees, Reverend Bauer. I'm not even sure I can add much to what the police will be doing."

"I still want you to try."

"All right."

Bauer looked down at his fists. He unfolded them slowly, as if they were unfamiliar objects whose workings he didn't quite understand. He looked down at his shirt, which had come untucked, and at his black suit coat, whose sleeves had ridden up over his forearms. He fussed with his clothes for a moment, then gave up.

"I'm a wreck. Give me a few minutes, will you? Go to the office. I'll meet you there. Olivia—Mrs. Seifert—can get you some coffee."

Bauer turned and bumped into the side of a pew. He put out his hands and felt his way around it, like a man moving in the dark. Free of it, he seemed to find his way. He crossed the front of the sanctuary with long strides and disappeared through a side door.

I glanced up at the stained-glass window with Jesus and the children. The lectern obscured most of the inscription from view. The only word I could see now was "Suffer."

$\triangledown$

Chapter 3

THERE WAS A MAN in the doorway of the church office, facing inward, his back to me. He was wearing a black T-shirt, cutoff jeans, and sandals. His posture, as he leaned against the doorjamb, conveyed a lazy insolence.

Over his shoulder I could see Mrs. Seifert, sitting at her desk, glaring at him. Or at something he held. A can of Budweiser.

"James Hadley," said Mrs. Seifert, shaking her finger at him as if she were scolding a child, "how dare you bring *that* in here?"

He laughed. "What's the big deal? Paul said, 'Take a little wine for thy stomach's sake.' I just happen to be out of wine at the moment."

"You know perfectly well that St. Paul was talking about drinking for medicinal purposes."

"Well, that's all right then, 'cause I am sick. Sick to death of this town." There was no humor in the man's voice, just bitterness. "Come right down to it, I'm sick of everything."

"You know why that is, don't you. You've turned away from the Lord and . . ."

"Spare me the Christian bullshit, will you, Olivia. You sure my father isn't around here somewhere?"

"I've already told you he isn't. Thank God for that, too. Thank God he doesn't have to see you like this."

"Are you kidding? He'd love it. Give him a chance to give me one of his sermons. That's about all I'd get too. I don't know why in hell I came here. That righteous skinflint would never help me out."

The man turned with impulsive abruptness, and I put out my hands to keep him from bumping into me. He bounced off my palms, sloshing some beer onto the faces on his Waylon-and-Willie T-shirt. He had a beard almost as thick as Willie's. He seemed to be in his late twenties. He said: "Shit, man, why don't you watch where you're going?"

For a moment there was a threat in his blue, watery eyes. Then he shrugged and was gone, his sandals making an angry flapping sound as he walked away.

"Who's that?" I asked Mrs. Seifert, as I went into the office.

"Jim Hadley. His father, Warren, is a wonderful man. A deacon. A member of the church board. How is it that good people can have such bad children?"

She spoke with vehemence. Her eyes were directed toward the hallway, but they were slightly glazed, and I suspected that she was really looking into her own past. I left her to her bitterness and went to the automatic coffee machine to get a cup of coffee. It was bitter too.

"Did you find Reverend Bauer?" asked Mrs. Seifert, as I sat on the straight chair in front of her desk. She was a thin woman, probably in her seventies, deeply tanned, with white hair cut short and close to her head, like a bathing cap.

"Yes. He's washing up. He asked me to wait for him here."

"How did he seem to you?"

"Not good."

Mrs. Seifert nodded. "It's terrible to see him so sad. It doesn't seem fair that someone so good should have such troubles. Sometimes it seems like the Lord sends the hardest trials to the best of his people. But Reverend Bauer tells us that the Lord doesn't promise Christians an easy life; He only promises to give us the strength to handle what comes.

Maybe that's the answer. The Lord knows the best Christians can handle more than the rest of us."

Mrs. Seifert seemed to look at me for confirmation. I've given up being indulgent about the sermons people toss at me. But I didn't want to be rude to her either. I just said: "It must be pretty rough for him. His son's been gone for . . . what? . . . Three days?"

"Yes. And he loves that boy so much. It's kind of amazing when you think of all the trouble that boy's given them." She paused, as if calculating the sum of trouble. "People are still talking about that one outburst in church. It was shocking. Mrs. Bauer was furious. She practically dragged the boy out of there. I felt so embarrassed for Reverend Bauer, standing up at the pulpit. But he didn't look embarrassed at all. He said: 'Please excuse my son. He can't help some of the things he says. He needs our prayers.' And then he went on with his sermon. He's such a good man." Mrs. Seifert's face glowed as she spoke of the minister.

"What's wrong with Billy?"

She looked startled. "You don't know about him?"

"No."

"Oh, dear. Sometimes I get talking and my mouth just works too fast for my head."

"What about Billy?"

She shook her head. "I think Reverend Bauer should be the one to tell you about that."

Mrs. Seifert looked down at her desk determinedly. On the edge of her desk was a plastic cube filled with pictures of cats. She reached out and gave the cube a quarter turn, changing cats as if she were changing subjects. I didn't want to stop her talking, so I said: "Tell me about Reverend Bauer. How old is he?"

"Fifty-three."

"He looks older than that."

"I suppose he does."

"He looks like he's had a hard life."

"Oh, he has. He was quite a sinner once. He'd be the first one to tell you that. Drinking, fighting, gambling, fornicating." She spoke the words with a certain innocent relish, like a housewife repeating the adventures of her favorite soap opera character. "He lost his job, his family, his health. He says he sunk about as low as a man can get. Then he found the Lord." She smiled happily at the conclusion of her story.

"So Billy and Mrs. Bauer are his second family?"

"That's right. After Reverend Bauer was saved, he went looking for his wife and two girls. But his wife had remarried and his girls really loved their new stepfather. Reverend Bauer thought it would be best for them if he didn't come back into their lives. It was a hard decision for him, but I guess it was all part of the Lord's plan. Mrs. Bauer is the perfect wife for a minister. She's such a strong Christian, and she works so hard for the church. Everybody admires her so much. Reverend Bauer too. He tells people he hopes one day he'll be as good a Christian as she is." Mrs. Seifert smiled indulgently. "Of course, he's just being modest. He . . . oh, here he comes now."

There were sounds of approaching footsteps, and Bauer appeared at the door. His hair was combed, his suit and shirt smoothed. His face had the ruddiness of a cold water rinse; his once red eyes were now a stark, eye-drop white. But none of the cosmetic changes hid the slump of his shoulders or the look of deep exhaustion in his face.

He exchanged a few halfhearted pleasantries with Mrs. Seifert while she got him a cup of coffee. Then he led me to his inner office, shutting the door behind us. The room was filled with comfortable-looking old furniture and uncomfortable-looking old books—books whose titles had words like "Moabite" and "Paleographic." There was a large picture window looking out on orange groves and a patch of cloudless sky.

I sat in an easy chair as Bauer went to his desk. At the center of the desk was a book entitled *Your God Can Do Miracles*. Bauer fingered the book for a moment, the way a smoker fingers a pack of cigarettes when he's trying to cut down. Then he pushed it aside.

My eye was drawn to a photograph in a polished silver

frame on a corner of the desk. It was a photo of a young boy, wearing a Dodgers cap that was tilted back on his face. The boy had a round face, high cheekbones, and a short nose, making him look slightly like a chipmunk. He was grinning at something off camera that he seemed to find hilarious.

"That your boy?" I asked.

"Yes. That's Billy."

"He looks like a nice kid. He looks happy."

Bauer took his time answering. "I guess he was then."

"What's he laughing at? Something your wife was doing?"

Bauer looked bewildered. "My wife? Oh, I see. No. I was with him. I was making faces. He liked those. Especially my gorilla imitation."

Bauer's roughed-up face filled with sudden tenderness, like a jagged creek bed flooded with a warm stream.

"I understand he's been missing since Monday. No one has any idea what happened?"

"No." Bauer was still staring at his son's picture. He reached out a large hand and wrapped it around the frame in a protective gesture.

"How old is Billy?"

"He's five. Almost six. He just finished kindergarten. This summer he's been spending a lot of time with Mrs. Tate at her day-care center. She's taken care of Billy on and off for years. She's very good with him. He loves her a lot."

Bauer drifted off into a reverie. I asked: "Where was your son last seen?"

"Pardon?" said Bauer, blinking at me like someone just waking from a nap.

"I said: Where was Billy last seen?"

"Sorry. It was at home. Martha—my wife—picked him up from Mrs. Tate's at three-thirty. Martha's been working on a fund-raising campaign for the church, and she's been pretty busy. She gave Billy a snack, then sent him out into the yard to play. She went to check on him later, and he was gone. She wasn't worried at first, just annoyed. She'd told him to stay in the yard, and she thought he'd wandered off. But then she couldn't find him, and none of the neighbors had seen him, and she began to get frightened. I've never seen her as frightened as she was that day."

"Then she called the police?"

"She called me. I was here in my office, working on my sermon. I did some looking myself, then I called the police. They began checking the neighborhood, and we organized a search party from the neighborhood and the church. We spent most of the night and the next day searching. We found no sign of Billy. None. The poor little guy . . ." Bauer's voice caught. He took a breath and squeezed his eyes shut. "I'm sorry."

"Take your time."

"Do you have any children?"

"No."

"It's terrible when something happens to one of your own. It's as if it's happening to you. To the most frightened part of yourself. On top of that it feels like it's your fault for not protecting them."

"I know."

"I thought you said you didn't have any children."

"I don't anymore. I did once. About Billy: No one saw him wander off?"

Bauer looked at me for a moment before answering. "No. The police questioned everyone. They asked if the neighbors had seen any strangers. Someone did see a pickup truck with some kind of work tools. Someone else saw a Volkswagen that was an odd orange color. That was all. The police are trying to check on the vehicles."

"I suppose the police told you that most missing children are either custody cases or runaways. Billy is your and your wife's natural son?"

"Yes."

"Is there anyone else who would feel he or she had a right to Billy?"

"No. Absolutely not."

"Five would be pretty young for a runaway, but it isn't impossible. Is there any reason you can think of why Billy would want to run away?"

"No," said Bauer, but his face looked a lot less certain than his answer.

"Do you want to modify that?"

Bauer took a long breath. "Billy has had problems. And he and my wife don't . . . But I can't believe it. Sure, he might go for a few hours to get attention. But three days—a five-year-old? Even if he had wanted to keep going, surely someone would have noticed him by now. And called the authorities. The police have notified all the agencies around here."

"You're probably right. Speaking of the police, I'll need to talk to them. I understand that Azalea has its own force. Who's in charge of the case?"

"Chief Wernecke. Azalea has a pretty small force—just a chief, a couple of sergeants, and a few officers. The chief handles anything of importance himself."

"I'll need a good photograph of Billy."

Bauer's hand tightened on the framed picture, as if he were afraid I'd try to take it from him. "Come to the house. I can get you one there."

"All right. I'd like to talk to your wife. Is she there now?"

Bauer hesitated. "She's there. But I'm not sure she'll talk to you."

"Why not?"

"For the sorts of reasons we talked about earlier."

"Can I try?"

"Yes. But on one condition. If she says no, that's that. I won't have you pushing at her the way you pushed at me." There was a glint of anger in Bauer's eyes.

"I suppose I should apologize for that."

"There's no need. You said what you felt. And I made up my own mind. But I won't have you pushing at her."

"Agreed."

"One other thing. If she does agree to talk to you, I want you to keep it brief. My wife is a very strong person, but sometimes she tries to be too strong. She keeps too much inside her. Outwardly she seems very calm, but I can see signs that this is affecting her deeply. I saw how frightened she was for Billy that first day."

"I'll keep it brief."

"All right, then. Let's go."

But Bauer didn't move right away. He lifted up his son's picture and stared at it intently, as if hoping to find some clue in it to where the boy was, or how he was. "Dear God," he whispered, "let him be safe." Then he slowly placed the picture back on the corner of his desk, next to the book on miracles.

$\bigtriangledown$

Chapter 4

Bauer pushed open the front door of the church. The glare hit us first, then the heat, like a noiseless explosion going off in our faces.

We stepped outside. Sunglasses took care of the glare, but nothing could take care of the heat, not here in the open. Sweat started dripping along my rib cage.

Ahead of us, across the street, was a single row of tract houses, without trees, against a background of farmland. The cramped houses seemed to run together, like objects melted and fused by the sun.

We turned left on the sidewalk, walking along the edges of the church lawn, which had begun to brown in the heat. The church was a sprawling, white frame building, set back from the street on a lot that had been carved out of the orange groves behind it. On the lawn was a large, glass-enclosed sign with movable letters that said "Azalea Bible Church" and announced the times of the various services. One line said, "The Reverend Vernon Bauer will speak on," and the rest was left blank, as if he had run out of things to say.

We stopped in front of a white frame house that appeared to be an extension of the church complex. Bauer had his hand on the gate of the white picket fence when we heard a metallic crash and a child's cry.

15

Across the street a young girl had tumbled from her bicycle. She was trying to sit up and push away the bike, which had fallen over her legs. I got to her first and knelt next to her, as Bauer knelt on the other side of the bike. For an ugly instant I couldn't see the whole of one of her legs, but then I understood the illusion. The lower part of her left leg was in a metallic brace that had seemed to blend with the bicycle. I slid her out, taking care to support the braced leg.

"You okay?" I asked.

"Yeah," she said, in a voice more angry than hurt. "That dumb brace!"

I heard another cry and looked up to see a young woman in shorts and a halter top running down the steps of the house just in front of me. "What are you doing to her?" she screamed. "You leave her a—Reverend Bauer?" She slowed as she saw the minister, then looked at the girl. "Julie, what—?"

"Relax, Charlene," said Bauer. "Everything's all right. Julie just took a little spill. She seems to be fine. Aren't you, Julie?"

"Yeah, yeah," said the girl, with an air of bravado that said, Don't fuss over me.

But the woman fussed anyway. I lifted Julie up and the woman took her, checking her face, her limbs, her brace, and her yellow shorts and top, questioning her in a voice laced with a slight Appalachian twang, while Julie whined, "Momma, I'm *okay*." The total damage seemed to be one slightly skinned knee and one slightly torn pair of shorts. When Julie was set free, she gave the bike tire a disgusted kick. I laughed and set the bike up on the sidewalk.

"Thanks," said the woman, looking at Bauer, then at me.

"Glad to help," I said, struggling to suppress a grin. This woman had the body of a centerfold, the freckled face of a tomboy, and a head full of absurdly tight red-brown curls with a single curler dangling from one side. The effect was ridiculous—and completely charming.

"I'm sorry I yelled at you," she said. "I didn't see Reverend Bauer at first. I just saw you with Julie, and I didn't know you, and we're all so scared after what happened to—"

The woman bit at her lip, cutting off the rest of the sentence. Her daughter moved up close to her. They both stared at the minister with solemn, embarrassed expressions, like two people who'd just stumbled onto a funeral.

"We shouldn't be troubling you like this," said the woman, tugging at her halter top.

"It's all right," said Bauer gently. "I'm just glad Julie's okay. Oh, by the way: This is Mr. Strickland. Mr. Strickland, Mrs. Benton and her daughter Julie. Mr. Strickland's a private detective."

At the mention of my profession, the girl's face brightened and the mother's face darkened. When Bauer added that I'd been hired to find Billy, the mother looked relieved.

"Are you a friend of Billy's?" I asked Julie.

"Un-huh," said the girl, with an earnest expression.

"I might want to come talk to you sometime. Would that be all right? Mrs. Benton?"

"Sure," said the mother, with no hesitation. "Anything we can do to help."

Bauer and I said our good-byes and walked back across the street. We walked up the steps of the white frame house, and Bauer opened the unlocked front door.

"Martha, I'm home," he called. "I have someone with me."

I blinked against the darkness of the front hallway. There was a living room to the left and a dining room to the right, and both rooms had thick, pulled shades that blocked out most of the light. The air was cool and slightly damp from an air conditioner that hummed somewhere. I felt as if I had just entered a cave.

There was a woman in the living room, sitting on a couch by a lit reading lamp, holding a Bible in her lap. She was looking toward us, but the lamp was behind her, and I couldn't quite make out her features. She looked quite elderly.

But in the ten or twelve steps it took me to cross the room, the woman dropped thirty years. In reality, she was at least ten years younger than Bauer. The impression of age had come from the stoop of her shoulders, the stiff way she held her body, and her near-anorexic thinness.

Bauer approached her with nervous deference. "Martha,

this is Mr. Strickland. He's . . . the detective Frank Edmundson sent us."

"How do you do," said Mrs. Bauer formally, as she gave me a sharp look. She turned to her husband. "I assume you told Mr. Strickland that we wouldn't be needing him."

Bauer took a deep breath. "No. I'm sorry. I've changed my mind. I want his help."

Anger darted in and out of her eyes like an animal at its burrow. As if she'd seen it, and was frightened, she hunched forward. Her voice was soft, almost timid, as she said: "I thought we'd agreed."

"We did. But I'm just not sure enough we're right. I can't presume to know what the Lord wants me to do. I don't want to make a mistake, not with Billy's life."

Mrs. Bauer looked down at the Bible in her lap, as if trying to read there what she should do. "I think you're wrong. But you're my husband, and I'll abide by your decision."

Bauer seemed enormously relieved. "Have a seat, Mr. Strickland. Martha, I'm going to get him a picture of Billy. I'll just be a minute."

As Bauer left the room, I took a seat on an ornate, straight-backed chair next to Mrs. Bauer's side of the old-fashioned couch. She straightened her shoulders and looked me in the eye, a slightly grim expression on her face. There was nothing timid about her now. She reminded me a little of a Sunday-school teacher I'd once had, a woman formidable because she was so sure she was right.

On the wall above Mrs. Bauer was a picture of Jesus. This was not the pleasant, pastel Jesus of the church windows; this was the grim, gaunt Jesus of thorns and scourges. Somehow that Jesus and Mrs. Bauer seemed a match. I suspected that she was an ascetic. The stiffness about her seemed to be that of determined control.

"Apparently you've convinced my husband that he'd do better to trust you than the Lord."

"I wouldn't put it quite that way."

"Where are you from, Mr. Strickland?"

"I work in the San Jose area."

"Is business a little slow there? I was just wondering what would get a sophisticated city detective like yourself to come all the way out to the Valley to a little hick town like Azalea."

She spoke with a straight face, but the sarcasm was obvious enough. The woman I wasn't supposed to be pushing seemed to be doing a bit of pushing herself. I said: "To tell the truth, I didn't exactly jump at the job. The San Joaquin Valley isn't my favorite part of California, least of all in July. But Frank Edmundson did me a favor once, and I owe him one. This is it. And he practically begged me to come. He seems to care about all of you a great deal."

That brought her up short. Her face softened and she patted at her short, wavy, brown hair, as if Edmundson's arrival were imminent. "Mr. Edmundson is an important man. Before he moved away, he was a leader of our church. He's been—he still is—very generous to us. And it's kind of him to concern himself with our family troubles. I wouldn't want him—or you—to think my reluctance to have you here is in any way personal."

"I didn't take it personally."

"I'm glad."

"I'm sorry about your son, Mrs. Bauer."

"Thank you. But Billy's in God's hands. Whatever happens to Billy will be the Lord's will."

That wasn't the greatest expression of mother love I'd ever heard. But this was a certain sort of Christian mother love, and that was something different. As I knew from experience.

"As long as I'm here, Mrs. Bauer, would you mind answering a few questions for me?" When she didn't respond right away, I said: "I know you don't want me here, but won't you humor me a little for your husband's sake? And for Frank Edmundson's. I know you're trusting in God to help you. But, honestly, I'll try not to get in His way."

She laughed and, for an instant, another thirty or more years rolled away, leaving a prim and proper young girl, taught not to laugh, hiding her laughter with the back of her hand as someone—perhaps a rogue uncle on an obligatory family visit—couldn't resist teasing her. For the first time I noticed that she had a pretty face.

"I'm sure you won't be in His way, Mr. Strickland," she said, still smiling. She closed and put aside her Bible, with the air of someone putting away a weapon that won't be needed. "All right. Ask your questions."

"That afternoon Billy disappeared, what time did you get him from the day-care center?"

"Three-thirty."

"And then?"

"I gave him some milk and crackers and sent him out to the backyard to play."

"What time did you check on him?"

"I'm not sure exactly. Maybe an hour later. Then an hour or so after that. Normally I would have checked on him more often, but I was feeling pretty pressed with some work I was doing. This has always been a safe neighborhood—nice people, no traffic, few strangers. Anyway, the first time I looked he was there. Making a fort for his toy soldiers."

"And the second time he was gone?"

"Yes. I'd told him to stay in the yard. My first thought was that he'd disobeyed me and gone off to play with some other children. Billy's been difficult lately."

"But you couldn't find him."

"No." She looked down at her empty hands. They were trembling slightly. Perhaps her husband was right. Perhaps her coldness—what he'd called her "strength"—was partly a veneer.

"Who are Billy's special friends around here?"

"He didn't have many in the neighborhood. Most of the children are much older. Except Julie."

"The little girl with the brace."

"You've met her?"

"A few minutes ago. And her mother. They seemed very nice."

"I don't know the mother very well," said Mrs. Bauer. "She's not a member of our church. She's a cocktail waitress." Her mouth formed an expression of distaste.

"Were there favorite places Billy liked to go? You know, places to explore, to hide, to play."

Mrs. Bauer took a long time to answer. "The woods."

"Back there?" I asked, pointing toward the far end of the living room.

When she nodded, I got up and walked to the end of the room. I pushed the fringed curtain and the shade aside, and looked out. There was a small backyard, enclosed by the fence that encircled the house. There was a back gate. Beyond the gate were trees—not the orange groves, but natural woods, mostly oak trees with a thick underbrush. It was impossible to see more than ten or twenty yards.

"Is your backyard visible from the house next door?"

"No. The trees block the view."

"What's back there? Besides trees, I mean."

"The lake." She spoke the word almost in a whisper. I could understand why. A boy lost in that would be lost forever.

Bauer came back into the room. He took one look at his wife, then rushed up to her, taking her hand in one of his. I let the shade fall back and went over to them. Bauer pushed two pictures at me with his free hand, while still looking at his wife, as if he were bribing me to go away.

One picture was a smaller copy of the one in Bauer's office. The other showed the boy standing in front of the church, dressed in a blue suit and bow tie, holding the hand of a woman whose face wasn't shown. The boy looked a little older and much thinner than in the first picture. He was staring to one side, and his face had a faraway look. Whatever he was seeing wasn't making him happy. In fact, I'd rarely seen eyes so sad on someone so young.

"Is there anything about Billy I should know?" I asked.

Bauer glanced toward the pictures in my hand, as if suspecting he'd given me the wrong one by mistake.

"No," said Mrs. Bauer firmly. "No."

Bauer had his mouth half-open, as if to speak. He and his wife stared at each other for a moment, their eyes locked. I had the feeling that they were engaged in a contest of wills. Finally Bauer shrugged and pressed his lips together. Apparently she had won.

$\triangledown$

Chapter 5

BAUER TOOK ME OUTSIDE. On the porch he stopped me with a hand to my shoulder. He leaned close, whispering, like a conspirator.

"There is more I need to tell you about Billy. But not here. Not now. Have you found a place to stay?"

"Frank made reservations for me at a place called the Garden Inn."

"I'll call you there later. I want to spend some time with Martha. Then I'd better lie down. I haven't had much sleep. I'm feeling pretty rocky."

"All right. Meanwhile I'd like to talk to Mrs. Tate. How about giving me directions to the day-care center?"

Bauer looked as glum and hesitant as if I'd asked him for a loan. But he gave me the directions and said: "Maybe it is just as well you'll be talking to her. She can tell you about Billy. I'm not sure I'm up to going through all that with you."

I left Bauer standing on the front porch, looking like something that had wilted in the heat. I wasn't feeling too energetic myself. Across the street a couple of kids were running back and forth through a lawn sprinkler, yelling and giggling. I gave them an envious glance as I headed for my car.

It took me about five minutes to find the day-care center. I pulled up to the curb next to a fence painted with cartoon animals with huge grins. Just outside my passenger window was a lion with a top hat and cane. He was giving me a smile and a wink, as if he had just told me a bawdy joke.

I walked up to the two-story red-brick house and rang the bell. The bell chimes played the first line of "Twinkle, Twinkle, Little Star." After a moment a woman answered the door. She had the same round face and big smile as the cartoon characters, though her smile looked a little tired. She was a big-boned, blond woman with ruddy skin. She was carrying a child in diapers, a little girl with her thumb in her mouth.

"Yes?"

"Mrs. Tate?" I asked. When she nodded, I told her who I was and asked if she could give me a few minutes.

"I don't know," she said. "Vern didn't say anything about you to me."

"I just left him at his house. He's the one who told me how to find you. You could call him. He did say he was going to take a nap, but he shouldn't be asleep yet."

Her look of indecision changed to a look of tenderness. "I hope he does get some sleep. He needs it. He looked awful the last time I saw him." She glanced behind her. "Come in, if you like. I don't mind talking, if you don't mind some competition. A few of the children haven't been picked up yet."

The entire downstairs of the house had been made over for children. There were shelves and boxes filled with toys and books. The walls were hung with sketches and finger paintings, most of them showing suns and trees and flowers and stick people. The floors were covered with dark, heavy-duty carpeting, and the furniture was all miniature tables and chairs. I felt like Gulliver among the Lilliputians.

I followed Mrs. Tate to a side room where three kids were playing. Two girls, looking rather prim in granny dresses, were engaged in a game of Old Maid. Nearby a boy was making engine and crash noises as he pushed two cars over the rug. Mrs. Tate looked around the room with a frustrated air.

"I'm not sure I have a chair that'll hold you," she said. "I'd invite you into the kitchen, but I need to keep an eye on them."

"I don't mind the floor."

She smiled. "All right, then. That would be easiest."

Mrs. Tate did a sort of curtsy that ended with her slipping easily to the floor, all the while holding the little girl. I got there with a lot less grace. Mrs. Tate sat facing me, her legs curled under the long paint-stained smock she wore. She put the little girl on her lap and handed her a miniature book.

"I understand you've been taking care of Billy for some time," I said.

"On and off since he was two. I've come to feel awfully close to him. Almost as if he were one of my own."

"Three years is a long time."

"Yes. But it's not just the length of time. I've had other children that long. It's that Billy's so . . . needy. That's hard for me to resist in a child. He's had such a rough time of it, and he needs love so badly, and he's grateful for any he gets. It just about kills me to think of him out there . . . in trouble. Why him? It's just not fair. Not after all he's been through."

There was a sudden commotion behind her. One of the card-playing girls was screaming, "Mrs. Tate, Mrs. Tate," as if the woman were in the next room rather than right there with her.

Mrs. Tate turned toward the girl. "Pipe down, Sylvia. What is it?"

"Tony took one of our cards. Tell him to give it back."

"Big deal!" said the boy. "I got the right to play with the cards if I want to."

Mrs. Tate lifted the toddler from her lap to the floor, then started crawling toward the argument, looking like a big toddler herself. "Tony, the girls had those cards first. You can't just . . ."

The little girl in diapers watched her caretaker moving away and seemed about to cry. Then she glanced in my direction and changed her mind. She got to her feet and toddled toward me, holding her open book in front of her by a single page. She plopped down in my lap and opened the book. The book seemed to have about ten pages, each showing an animal covered with fuzz. The girl poked, then stroked, then punched each animal in a methodical sequence, as if only in that way could she appreciate the true meaning of the story. Each time she turned a page she glanced back and up at me, making sounds I couldn't understand.

"I see you're getting read to," said Mrs. Tate, as she crawled back. "You want me to take her?"

"She's all right where she is."

"You have any children?"

"No."

"You should," she said, as she resumed her cross-legged position. "You're a natural."

I glanced down at the child and started to crack a joke, but suddenly the temperature of the room seemed to drop. With the cold came a feeling of dread, that this child was too delicate a thing to be entrusted to me. I knew the feeling was irrational, but it was too strong to shake off easily. I didn't want to fight with it, not here among strangers.

"Maybe you had better take her," I said. Carefully, and as gently as I could, I lifted the girl up and handed her over to Mrs. Tate.

"Is something wrong?" The woman's eyes searched my face as she took the child.

I tried a laugh to reassure her. "No. I just get nervous sometimes holding little kids. They seem so fragile."

"They're not," she said, giving me an indulgent look. "You'll understand that when you have some of your own." But then, as if she'd been infected by my mood, her face turned sad. "Some of them are, though."

"You mean Billy?"

"Yes."

"What's wrong with Billy? I've gotten lot of hints that something's wrong with him, but no one's told me what it is."

Mrs. Tate started stroking the head of the girl she held. "Billy's got something the doctors call Tourette's syndrome. I'd never heard of it before, but I've come to find out it isn't all that rare."

"What is it?"

"It's pretty bizarre. But mostly it's just sad. Poor Billy.

About a year ago he stared getting . . . agitated. He started
having tics. Not just little facial twitches, but odd repetitive
movements. He'd do things like shaking his head back and
forth, or shaking his fist, or pounding on things. These episodes would go on for a little while, then stop. After that
Billy would be perfectly normal. I didn't know what to think.
I suggested to his parents that they take him to a neurologist
or a psychiatrist. But they wouldn't hear of it at first. Christians can be pretty backward when it comes to psychological
disorders."

"You're not a Christian?"

"No, I am. At least I consider myself to be one. In fact, a
born-again Christian. But I'm a lot more liberal than most
of the people at the church."

"You go to Azalea Bible?"

"Yes," she said, glancing down at the child in her lap, who
was falling asleep. "My late husband and I joined Azalea
Bible when we first came here from Wisconsin. I was a lot
more conservative then. But I've come to believe that being
a born-again Christian doesn't commit you to taking everything in the Bible as literal truth. It doesn't commit you to
taking science as your enemy. I've thought of switching
churches, but there isn't another one around here that suits
me better. Anyway, I like a lot of people at Azalea Bible. And
I like Reverend Bauer. He's a good man. A kind man. And
he preaches good sermons."

"I take it he and his wife don't share your attitude toward
science."

"Vernon's more liberal than Martha. But neither of them
is real liberal. Anyway, psychology's the tough one for Christians to handle. We're used to thinking of mental problems
in spiritual terms. Things to be handled through religion,
not medicine."

"So what did they do about Billy?"

Mrs. Tate's face took on a pained look. "They came down
pretty hard on him. Discipline. Sermons. They thought Billy
was just being difficult. Doing things to spite them. To be
fair, they weren't without some justification. You see, Billy

does have some control over his symptoms. That threw us all off in the beginning. But it turns out that the control he has is only temporary. So the discipline didn't work. It only made things worse for Billy. Martha was particularly hard on him. She's the real disciplinarian in that family. Vernon's pretty soft when it comes to kids." She smiled, and looked down at the sleeping child in her lap.

"Lucky for Billy he had you."

She shrugged. "I hope I made things easier for him. He was so starved for some understanding. Vern loves that boy very much. But he got confused by what was happening. Martha too."

"She didn't strike me as a particularly warm woman."

"Martha's a good woman," said Mrs. Tate emphatically. "I mean that. She works tirelessly for the church. She puts the Lord's work first in all things. She never asks anything for herself. A lot of people at the church think of her as a saint. But good people don't always make good parents. Or good . . ." Mrs. Tate cut the sentence short with a look of embarrassment.

"Wives?"

"I didn't say that," she said, sharply. "Don't put words in my mouth." She gave me a brief look of anger, then dropped her eyes and seemed to fidget. "I have to get the children ready."

She got to her feet, holding the little girl, and began directing the other children to put away cards and blocks. A few minutes later the door chimes rang and a vivacious young mother appeared. Mrs. Tate showed a certain regret as she let the little girl be taken from her. In another ten minutes two other mothers appeared to claim the auto racer and the two card players. Mrs. Tate showed no regret this time.

"You still angry?" I asked, from my place on the floor, when we were alone.

"No," she said, smiling, standing over me. "Anyway, I was really mad at myself. What you said was what I was thinking. But it's none of my business. And I shouldn't be so judgmental. I don't like that in myself." She seemed to accept

her own verdict, then shrug it off. "Come on. If you want to
talk some more, let's talk in the kitchen. I'll get you a cup
of tea. And a decent chair."

She reached down and helped me up with strength of arm
that surprised me. I followed her to a large country kitchen
at the far end of the house, a room with adult-sized table
and chairs. I felt like I was back in civilization again.

I did some stretching to get the kinks out of my lower back
while Mrs. Tate was making the tea. When we were both
seated at the table, I said: "I still don't feel like I'm all that
clear about Billy's condition. What was the name again?"

"Tourette's syndrome."

"You said it was bizarre. Someone else used the word
shocking. But I don't see what's so shocking and bizarre
about some repetitive movements."

"I haven't told you the worst of it," said Mrs. Tate through
the steam of the teacup she'd raised to her lips. She took a
tentative sip, found the tea too hot, and put the cup back
down on the flowered tablecloth. "The symptoms built up
slowly. That's typical of Tourette's. There were the facial
tics. Then odd sniffing noises. Then the repetitive movements. Then finally what they call coprolalia."

"Which is?"

"Violent outbursts of swearing. And what some people
would call blasphemy. Long, loud strings of awful words that
would go on and on, like random gestures, before they'd stop
and Billy would be Billy again. You can imagine the effect
that would have on any parents. But a minister and his wife?
They got pretty hysterical."

"Hysterical enough to take you up on your psychiatrist
suggestion?"

She gave a half nod. "Eventually. But the first people they
consulted were a rather elderly and out-of-date general prac-
titioner and a Christian counselor with a minimum of training. They were no help at all. Then Martha really started
going after Billy as if it were a test of wills, or a test of faith,
and that just made things worse, and Vern got desperate
enough to take me up on my suggestion. I'd gotten the name

of a very competent psychiatrist—Dr. Rodenbaugh—who's also a Christian. It's good he is a Christian; he was able to talk to Vern in his own language, to talk about the diagnosis in a way that Vern didn't find threatening. Dr. Rodenbaugh consulted with a neurologist, and they did some tests, and they said Billy had Tourette's. I'm still not as clear about the disease as I'd like to be, but they claim it's a matter of brain chemistry. Billy can put off his attacks temporarily, like I said. But in the end he just can't help himself."

I shook my head. "It isn't just Christians who get confused by psychiatry. Some of this stuff is pretty hard to follow. How does brain chemistry make someone swear?"

Mrs. Tate gave me a sympathetic look. "It is pretty confusing. But Dr. Rodenbaugh tried to explain it to me in simple terms, and it did make some sense. He said that prohibited words, because they have such emotional power, are stored in—I don't remember if he said more parts of the brain, or a special part of the brain. Anyway, he said that stroke victims who can barely utter a word can often swear clearly. That's because the brain paths involving the swear words are less likely to get blocked. That's sort of what happens to Billy. He gets under stress, and a lot of paths in his brain get blocked. Something has to come out. It's the swear words. Does that make sense to you?"

"I guess so. Is there any kind of treatment?"

"They give Billy something called Haldol. At first it stopped the symptoms all right, but at the cost of doping Billy up so badly he could barely function. So Dr. Rodenbaugh cut back on the dosage. He called it a compromise. Some attacks, though not so many, and more ability to function in between."

"Is there any kind of cure?"

Mrs. Tate shook her head slowly. "No. Most cases are for life. But sometimes the symptoms just go away. That's what we've been hoping and praying for with Billy."

"It sounds terrible for him."

"It is. But what makes it really terrible is the way other people react. Apparently the attacks don't feel awful to the

child who's having them. What feels awful is the way other
people react. People get confused and frightened by any kind
of irrational outburst. Add to that the fact that Billy's outbursts take the form of something that the people around
him judge in very strict moral terms and you have a terrible
situation. A lot of people treat him like he's a leper, or worse.
A lot of parents won't let their kids go anywhere near him.
Poor Billy has just been getting more and more frightened
and depressed."

"Mrs. Seifert mentioned something about an outburst in
church."

"Oh, that." Mrs. Tate's face screwed up as if she were in
physical pain. "It was horrible. Right in the middle of
church. Just before his father's sermon. Billy was sitting near
the front with his mother, and suddenly he started screaming
things. 'Fucking Jesus shit fuck God shit . . .' On and on."
Mrs. Tate was staring beyond me, as if the scene were there
in the distance. Then she squeezed her eyes shut and took
a deep breath. "It was unbelievable. Most of the congregation
didn't know about Billy before that. His parents had kept
him away from church when his attacks started getting bad.
They only brought him back when the medication made it
safe. Only this was when Dr. Rodenaugh had started cutting
back on the medication. Anyway here's this boy screaming
these horrible things at the top of his lungs, and three hundred churchgoers staring at him in shock. Martha was furious. She dragged him out of there while he was
screaming—and I mean dragged. After a few minutes I got
worried and went outside. Billy had gotten over his attack
and now it was his mother who was screaming. It took me
awhile to get her calmed down."

A trickle of perspiration appeared at the side of her face.
She wiped it away with the side of her hand. "Vernon was
wonderful about it. He kept calm and explained to the congregation that Billy had a medical problem and couldn't help
the things he said. That helped a bit, but not all that much.
Some people were understanding. Others decided that he was
a horrible little boy. Some decided that he was possessed."

"Possessed? By a devil?"

"That's right."

"Good God. This isn't the backwoods of Tennessee."

Mrs. Tate looked at me for a moment. Then her mouth formed an ironic smile. "Are you a Christian?"

"I assume you mean 'born-again Christian.' If I remember correctly, born-again Christians always talk as if they're the only kind of Christian."

"I suppose we do."

"I thought I was born again once. I'm not any kind of Christian anymore."

"Back when you were, did you believe in God as a spirit?"

"Yes."

"Angels? A guardian angel? That sort of thing?"

"I was taught that, yes."

"A devil who tempted people?

"Yes."

"And fallen angels who assisted the devil the way the good ones assisted God?"

"I guess so."

"Were you brought up in the backwoods of Tennessee?"

I laughed. "New Jersey. Though sometimes that seemed pretty strange."

"What you believed are the standard things that born-again Christians believe. That there are good and bad spirits who influence what people do. Is it such a big step to think that one of the bad spirits might influence someone in an extreme way? That's all demonic possession is. It doesn't seem to me such a big step from those other beliefs. In any case, it is clearly in the Bible."

I shook my head, resisting the last few steps in her religious logic. Watching me, she said: "Don't misunderstand me. These people aren't kooks. They're your ordinary doctors, lawyers, plumbers, whatever. They don't hold secret meetings where they conduct strange rites. They don't handle snakes. And they don't practice rites of exorcism. I just want you to realize that believing someone's behavior could be influenced by a devil isn't that extreme for a Christian."

I was silent for a few moments, mulling something over as I took a few swallows of the dark, rich tea. Then I asked: "Is it possible that someone might be driven to hurt Billy because he thinks Billy's possessed?"

"No," she said. "Not these people. What I've been trying to say is that they are not extreme in their behavior. Anyway you wouldn't identify the person with the devil, and you wouldn't want to hurt the person." She was speaking and gesturing with animation. But then some of the energy seemed to run out of her denial. Her hands dropped to the table. "Look, I suppose anything is possible. But it's also possible that someone outside the Church was simply frightened by Billy's behavior and struck out at him."

"So Tourette's syndrome and Billy's disappearance could be connected."

"Yes. There's one possibility I can't seem to get out of my thoughts." Her voice was almost a whisper.

"What's that?"

"Billy's been awfully depressed the last few months. He's been in therapy for that, but I'm not sure how much good it's been doing. What can it do really? It won't change the way people treat him. And the medicine he takes has a depressive effect." Her shoulders slumped, as if she were sharing the boy's condition. "I've been having this dream lately. It has to do with quicksand. I used to dream of quicksand a lot as a child—maybe from all those jungle movies they used to show. Only in this dream I have now it's Billy who's in the quicksand. I'm at the edge, and I'm reaching out my hand, and he's close enough so I could get hold of him, pull him out, if he'd just put out his hand to me. But he won't. He says, 'I'm tired, Lizzie. I want to die.' "

It took me a moment to understand what she was saying. "You're suggesting suicide? A five-year-old boy?"

"Yes," she said. "Though not by obvious adult means. I'm talking about a depressed child taking risks until something terrible happens." Her eyes scanned my face. "Don't kid yourself, Mr. Strickland. Children do commit suicide. We don't hear about it because no one wants to admit it. The parents certainly don't want to know; their guilt would be unbearable. I guess none of us want to think of creatures so helpless having such despair. We want to cling to our fantasies of childhood as a happy time, despite all the evidence to the contrary. And because children's suicides look so much like accidents, they're easy to explain away. But the people who study such things say that children do kill themselves. Even very small children."

"And you think Billy . . . ?"

"I don't know. It's just a possibility, a thought I can't get out of my head."

"But you think he was unhappy enough for that?"

"Yes," said Mrs. Tate. "I do."

$\triangledown$

Chapter 6

I LEFT THE DAY-CARE center and drove toward town. The tract houses began to thin out, giving way to fields full of dust and dead grasses. "Lot for Sale" signs stood along the roadside like so many beggars.

One parcel of land had been scorched by a brush fire. The fire was long dead, but the heat and the haze and the glare gave the illusion that all the land was burning.

I saw what appeared to be four children running across a field. I kept glancing at them, amazed that anyone could move that fast in the heat. Then the children seemed to grow into teenagers, and I saw that three of them were chasing the fourth. The one being chased was wearing a white shirt, the shoulder of which was covered with blood.

They were ahead, to the right, moving away from me. I stepped on the gas and found a dirt track that crossed the field. My car bounced over the rutted track, overtaking, then passing, the runners, fifty yards to the side of them. I noticed that the one in front was running hunched over. Then I saw why. One of the pursuers was throwing rocks at him.

I was hoping for another track that would cross in front of them, but I couldn't find one. I skidded to a stop and got out, coughing against the dust of the skid. I started running across the field. I could see now that the one being chased wasn't a teenager at all, but a short, slender man. The blood on his shirt came from a wound at the side of his head.

The man hesitated when he saw me coming, but I yelled something encouraging, and he veered toward me. I passed him and took a collision course toward the others. I got glimpses of meaty young faces, football haircuts, jeans, and sweat-soaked T-shirts. I yelled, "Leave him alone," and one of them yelled back, "Bullshit."

Two of them moved to either side of me, to get around, like two receivers splitting in front of a defender. The biggest one went to my left. I took a couple of steps toward him and kicked him hard in the knee. He went down with a groan. The one coming at me threw a punch. I sidestepped it and hit him in the nose. I turned to see where the third had gone, and just as I turned he hit me with a high tackle, numbing my nose and mouth with the top of his head. I went down hard and lost my breath for an instant as the kid leaned back, his fist raised. Just then the man hit him across the back with a stick. I don't think that hurt the kid—it sounded too much like a slap—but it must have scared him. He started to roll away, to defend himself from the man, and I hit him a glancing blow to the neck.

I was scrambling to my feet, trying to locate all three of the teenagers, when I heard the siren. They'd heard it too and were heading back the way they'd come, one of them limping after the others.

I turned around and looked at the man standing just behind me. He was in his mid-thirties, about five-eight, with a soft, timid face and thinning brown hair. His baggy seersucker slacks were dirty and torn. An open hand was pressed against the wounded side of his face in a gesture of dismay.

"You all right?" I asked.

"I don't . . . know," he said. He was breathing hard, struggling to get the words out. "I . . . guess so."

"Let me look at your face." I pulled his hand away and examined the cut on his cheek. It was a couple of inches long, not deep, and had stopped bleeding. "It doesn't look too serious, but you'd better see a doctor. You're going to need a couple of stitches."

"Your lip's cut," he said.

Now that my mouth was less numb, I could feel the slit on my lower lip. I tested it with my finger. It didn't seem like much.

"Thanks for helping me, mister," he said. "Thanks a lot."

"It's okay. Thanks for hitting that guy. My mouth would have looked a lot worse if you hadn't."

"I couldn't just leave you there with them."

The man was now breathing normally. But his face was pale, and he was swaying slightly. I took his arm and helped him back toward the car. As we began to walk, he said, with bitterness, "They threw rocks at me—like I was some dog." But as we continued, his mood seemed to lift. "You showed them though; you sure did." A moment later he added, "I guess we both showed them," and he seemed almost happy.

However, his mood and body seemed to deflate as we got close to the dirt track. A black-and-white was parked next to my car. An officer was standing there, watching us with arms folded and legs spread apart, making no effort to come and help. When we were about ten feet away, the officer said: "Gettin' in trouble again, Henry?"

It was only as the officer spoke that I realized it was a woman. She was tall, maybe six feet, with broad shoulders and almost no hint of a bust under the blue uniform. Her blond hair was cut short as a man's, and her face aped the grim guardian look of so many male cops. The only visual clue to her gender was the soft, beardless jaw.

"It wasn't my fault," said Henry, in a whining voice. "Some guys jumped me and . . ."

"Yeah, I know," said the officer, in a bored, just-joking tone. "Your mother called us. It was Val and his buddies?"

"Yeah."

I took Henry to my car and leaned him against the fender. As the officer approached him, Henry's body made subtle movements of defense until she stopped a couple of feet away. She glanced at his cut, made the same comments about stitches that I had, then asked him a few questions.

I became suddenly conscious of my own sweat-soaked body. I began to feel dizzy and leaned against the car for a moment, lowering my head. The discomfort began to pass.

"You all right?" said the cop to me.

"Yeah. It's just this heat."

She laughed. "You'll get used to it."

"If I'm here that long." I looked up at the officer. "You know the names of those guys who jumped him?"

"Yeah."

"I assume you're going to arrest them."

The officer turned from me to Henry. As the two of them looked at each other, their faces made a series of moves and countermoves, as if in some game I didn't understand. Finally the officer said: "That what you want, Henry?"

Henry lowered his eyes like an intimidated child. His voice was both submissive and sullen as he said: "I don't want to cause trouble. But I don't want 'em coming after me again."

"They won't bother you again," said the officer. "I'll have a talk with them and their parents."

"You're going to give them a lecture?" I said. "For this? Why don't you get really tough and make them write 'I won't commit assault and battery' on the blackboard fifty times."

"What are you—his attorney?" said the officer, sarcastically. "How do you figure in this anyway?"

"He was driving by," said Henry. "He stopped and helped me out."

"A Good Samaritan, huh?" said the officer. She didn't make it sound like a compliment.

"Why are you going so easy on those boys?" I asked. "One of them the mayor's son?"

A look of anger came over the officer's face. She tried to cover it with a mask of sarcasm, but some of the red showed through.

"Okay, smartass," she said. "Let's see some ID."

I took my driver's license out of my wallet and handed it over. As she glanced at it, she got a glint of satisfaction in her eyes, as if she were a card-playing opponent and I'd just dealt her the card she needed to take away my money.

"Well, what'd you know. If it isn't Dick Tracy."

I hadn't shown her my investigator's license. Surprise must have shown on my face, and she obviously enjoyed that.

"There's not much goes on around here we don't know about, Strickland. By the way, the chief wants to see you. I'll see if now's convenient for him."

"What if now's not convenient for me?"

"That's your tough luck."

The officer—her name tag said "Dawson"—went over to the black-and-white and got on the radio. I turned to Henry. He was looking back and forth from Dawson to me, as jittery as an undersized kid who was afraid he was going to be forced to take sides in a schoolyard brawl.

"Press charges against those guys," I said. "I'll back you up."

Henry just shook his head.

"What's the matter?" I asked. "Is there something going on I don't know about?"

Henry shook his head again, but I didn't get the impression it was a denial. "Please, mister, just drop it. I appreciate what you did for me, but I can't afford any trouble. Really."

"Why not?" I asked, and got no answer.

Dawson came back to where we were standing. "The chief wants to see you now, Strickland. You follow me in your car. When we get through town, you'll see a water tower on your right. The station's the white building just below it. You stop there, and I'll take Henry to the hospital." Dawson paused, looking me over with her head cocked to the side, like a museum-goer trying to get a fix on a troublesome painting. "Strickland, you wouldn't get cute and miss your appointment, would you? Don't. You won't like it if we have to come get you. Let's go, Henry."

The drive to town took an uncomfortable ten minutes. The inside of my car was hot as an oven, with my broken-down air conditioner buzzing uselessly, sounding like an oven fan. Beads of sweat started dribbling over my face and chest, and I swatted at them as if they were insects attacking.

The empty fields became orange groves and ramshackle farmhouses, the yards of the houses having that peculiar rural clutter of farm implements, broken appliances, junk cars, rusty swing sets, and plastic wading pools. Then there were several packing plants and feed stores, clustered around a railroad spur; then several residential blocks of bungalows, set close together, separated by picket fences and maple trees and trim, tiny lawns.

The main part of town looked like something out of the Midwest, as did so many of these San Joaquin Valley towns that had been built by the railroaders. There were three blocks of boxy, two-story stone buildings built along a broad street with diagonally parked pickups, station wagons, and sedans, most of them American-made. The buildings had wooden awnings, thick as walls, suspended from the sides by cables, giving the illusion of being huge shutters and the impression that when the town closed down for the night, it would do so with a vengeance. The store signs I noticed said "Tru-Value," "Rexall," "Thrift Store," "Ice Cream," and "Pool/Beer."

I heard the patrol car honk just as I saw the water tower. I pulled to the curb next to the police station, a square, white, almost windowless building that looked like a giant salt lick. Inside I told the Hispanic receptionist who I was and what I wanted, and found out that the odd-looking building had once been a jail. I sat for twenty minutes in a brown plastic chair while my sweat slowly turned to chills in the polar air-conditioning, and then was shown into the chief's office.

Chief Wernecke was a heavyset man wearing a tan business suit, white shirt, and brown striped tie; a tan Stetson hung from a rack in the corner of the room. He had a round, flat face and heavy, drooping eyelids that gave him the look of a Buddha. But this Buddha gave the impression that he had spent his life contemplating not the infinite but the degenerate, had achieved not nirvana but a state of total cynicism.

As I entered the room, he leaned back in his swivel chair, looking me over. "You know, Strickland, when I call a private cop into my office to give him a lecture on staying out of trouble and he comes walking in with blood on his shirt, it don't look real encouraging, you know what I mean?"

I glanced down at myself. There were drops of blood on my shirt, tie, and sports jacket, though the blood was most obvious on the shirt, purple against the blue cloth. I started to give him an explanation, but he waved it away.

"Dawson told me about it. So you were playing Good Samaritan for Henry Tuttle, huh?" He seemed to find that amusing.

"You got a problem with that?"

"Not me," he said, smiling. "Some people might."

"Why's that?"

He shrugged off my question in favor of one of his own. "So, you gonna play Good Samaritan for me and show a hick cop how to handle the Bauer case?" The smile was still there, but the amusement was gone.

I knew that Wernecke was a graduate of several East Bay police forces, that he'd ended up a lieutenant in Oakland before taking the semi-retirement position as Azalea Chief of Police. I knew he was no hick, but I was in no mood to flatter him. Anyway, Oakland graduated both good and bad cops, and I didn't yet know which he was. Based on Dawson's performance, I wasn't optimistic.

I just said: "You wanted to see me?"

Wernecke scowled, perhaps because I wasn't playing his game.

"Did I *want* to see you?" he said. "Frankly, Strickland, you're about as welcome here as a turd in a punch bowl. You're the last thing I *wanted* to see. But you're in my bowl, and I got to deal with you."

We glared at each other for maybe thirty seconds. Then Wernecke gave a small sigh, as if he were an old actor who was becoming tired of a role he'd been playing for too long. He waved his hand impatiently toward a straight-backed chair in front of his desk.

"Sit down, Strickland, and stop glaring at me. It's possible I'm stuck with you, and you sure as hell are stuck with me. We might as well make the best of it."

As I sat down, Wernecke tilted his chair forward and put

his elbows on his desk pad. He picked up a pencil and gripped it with both fists, just in front of his jaw. He looked over it at me, as if it were the top of a wall separating us.

"Nothing personal, Strickland, but private cops aren't my favorite people. Normally, I find one nosing around in one of my cases, I harass his ass out of here. Frank Edmundson's got enough clout so that if he wants you here and vouches for you, that gets you in. It maybe even gets you a little bit of cooperation. But that's all it gets you. You get in my way, you hold out on me, you fuck with any of the rules, I'll make you a very sorry man. You got that?"

"Sure. You mean that only your own officers get to fuck with the rules."

Wernecke's jaw clenched just as the pencil in front of his face snapped, creating the odd illusion that he'd just bitten it in half. "What the hell are you talking about?"

I told him. I was taking a chance, but I was angry, and anyway I wanted to know what I was dealing with here. To my surprise he didn't get belligerent. He just looked disgusted.

"Those boys don't belong to anyone important," he said. "Wouldn't matter if they did." He glanced toward the window, chewing at the inside of one cheek. Then he looked back at me. "Contrary to the impression you got, Dawson's a good officer. Maybe she tries too hard to be one of the boys sometimes, but she's good. And she's fair. But she's not real fond of Henry Tuttle, and maybe she let her personal feelings get in the way on this one. I'll talk to her, and I'll talk to Henry. If he wants to press charges, then that's how it'll be. No pressure from us either way. Okay?"

"Okay."

"I'm not sure he'll want to, though," he said, softly, almost as an afterthought.

"Why not?"

"That's his business, Strickland. You're such a good friend of his, you can ask him yourself."

Wernecke gave me a hard look. I had the feeling he thought I'd gotten some advantage over him, and he didn't like it.

"Let's get back to you," he said. "Tell me what the fuck

you're doing here. Edmundson I can understand. He's rich, and rich guys think they ought to be able to handle any situation by throwing money at it—money and the things money can buy." He gave me a look that said I was one of those things. "But you—you ought to know better. This is no custody snatch or runaway kid. Unless you know something I don't—in which case you'd better hand it over damn fast—it looks like either the kid had an accident somewhere or got picked up by some kook. Either way—even though we're going through all the motions—it looks to me like a matter of waiting and keeping in touch with other agencies. I'm already paid to wait, and those other agencies wouldn't give you shit. You know all that."

"Yeah. I told Frank that. He wants me here anyway."

"So you decided what the hell, I'll make a little easy money, right?"

"Chief, sitting in this nowhere town in a-hundred-and-ten-degree heat isn't my idea of easy money."

"A hundred and two," said Wernecke. "And it's not a bad place."

I blinked at him. I didn't know what surprised me more, his shifting off our argument to defend his town, or the embarrassed softening of his face as he did so.

"What's this—the Chamber of Commerce?"

Wernecke shrugged. "I like this place, that's all. It's a clean town with good people. Doesn't have all the scum and psychos I had to put up with in the East Bay for thirty years. It's true the summer heat gets pretty bad, but you can be out of it in half an hour by heading up into the mountains." Wernecke jerked his thumb over his shoulder, as if the mountains were leaning up against his back wall. "I got a cabin up there—which I bought with the money I had left over after I sold that overpriced house in Oakland and bought a bigger house in Azalea. Cabin sits on a lake, my own dock in front. Got an old beat-up rowboat with a five-horsepower Evinrude. It ain't fancy, but it gets me and the gear and the beer out to where the fish are biting." Wernecke's face took on a glow.

"Does sound nice."

"It's the best. And it's where I'd have been all this week if it hadn't been for the Bauer case."

Wernecke gave a sigh and glanced down at his desk. He picked up the broken halves of the pencil and tossed them into the wastepaper basket. He glanced at his watch, then at me.

"Long as you're here, Strickland, I guess I can give you a few questions. If you're lucky, I might even give you a few answers."

This was what I'd been waiting for, and I had my questions ready.

"I gather from what you've said that you've got no leads on the boy's disappearance?"

"That's right. He's gone, that's all we know. And we've done everything we could to know more."

"Do you have any reason to suspect that someone from Azalea might have done something to the boy?"

Wernecke hesitated a moment, massaging his jaw with one hand. "We wondered about a couple of people. But we checked them out and there's no evidence that they're involved."

"Would you mind giving me their names?"

"Yeah, I mind. I told you we checked them out. I don't see any reason why I should get them bothered by you."

"Bauer mentioned that two vehicles were seen in the neighborhood—a pickup carrying some tools, and an orange VW. Any information on those?"

"The pickup belongs to a local landscaping service. The two guys in the truck were going from one job to another, and their time is accounted for. We got nothing on the orange VW bug. Far as I can tell, there isn't one in town. But there are enough of them in the county that just knowing the make and color won't do us any good. I have put the word out on it, though."

"Have you dragged the lake in back of Bauer's house?"

Wernecke just stared at me for a moment, then shook his head, his face glum. "No. I wanted the sheriff's department to have Search and Rescue drag the lake, but all they've been dragging so far is their feet. I guess I can see their side of it; it's going to be a hell of a job dragging a lake that size and they want to see some other possibilities ruled out first. Still . . . What are the other possibilities? I said it had to be either a kook or an accident, but we both know the kooks are pretty rare. My guess is that the boy wandered off, got in some kind of accident. Probably dead by now, though I wouldn't say that to his parents. If I'm right, where is he?" Wernecke glanced down at his desk top, his eyes moving back and forth, like a man looking for something on a map. "We searched the whole area pretty good after the boy disappeared. I don't say there couldn't be some well or cave or something we missed, but I don't think it's too likely. The more we searched, the more I thought about that lake. I'm still thinking about it. If I had to guess, I say that's where he is, poor kid. At the bottom of that lake."

▽

Chapter 7

IN MY DREAM ALL was black except for a thin line of white light around the edges of a door. I knew Katie was on the other side, and I knew that something was terribly wrong. I called, but she wouldn't answer; I threw myself against the door, but it wouldn't budge. Then I saw that the light around the door was turning blood red, and I started to scream.

I woke shaking and disoriented in what seemed like total darkness. Gradually the forms around me took shadowy shape, and I realized that I was in my motel room, sitting in a chair where I'd dozed off. The room was cold from the air conditioner. I hugged myself to dispel the chill.

I looked at the illuminated digital clock—it was 10:00 P.M.—and just then the phone buzzed. It was Bauer, asking if I still wanted to talk. I didn't want to see anyone, but I felt I had to see him. We agreed to meet in the motel dining room in half an hour. I took a hot shower, dressed, and left the room.

I couldn't shake the effects of the dream. It was as if I were still half-submerged in it, the fear of it spilling over into the commonplace world of motel corridor, stairs, and lobby.

I entered the candle-lit dining room. It was done in a garden motif, all green and white, with large potted plants on window ledges and vines growing up trellises that served as sectioning screens. It was all very ordinary, yet the flickering shapes and shadows seemed somehow malevolent.

I was shown to a table at the back of the room. I ordered a whiskey, fidgeting with the table setting and the menu until the drink came. Just as I reached for the glass, it began: the dizzy tilting of the world, the pressure on my chest that made it hard to breathe, the brain full of danger signals, the rush of terror.

I'd had these moments on and off since Katie's death. I knew what they were now, but knowing didn't help me control them. I took a gulp of the whiskey, then forced myself to put the glass aside, knowing that way would only lead to worse troubles. I closed my eyes, tried to breathe evenly, tried to relax myself, but mostly I just endured. It seemed to go on for an hour, though it couldn't have been more than ten minutes. Gradually it began to subside.

"Mr. Strickland, are you all right?"

I hadn't heard Bauer approach. He was standing by the table, leaning over, a hand on my forearm, studying my face. His eyes were kind, but he'd startled me, and I was feeling that rush of anger I always felt after those episodes. I yanked my arm away from his large hand.

"I'm fine," I said, in a hoarse voice.

Bauer showed no reaction to my rudeness. He took a chair across from me, folding his arms on the table. His clothing was more comfortable now—an open-necked dark blue sport shirt under a gray-and-blue sports jacket. His rough face had a more rested look.

"You're white as a sheet," he said. "Are you sick?"

"No. Not exactly."

His eyes shifted to the glass of whiskey, no doubt wondering if that was the source of my troubles. There was no condescension in his face as he studied the glass, rather something like awe. His fingers ran over the nose with the broken capillaries, as if testing an old wound that was still tender.

Even though he didn't seem condescending, his assumption that I had alcohol troubles struck a nerve that had been raw for almost as long as I'd been alive. Without meaning to, I said: "It's not booze—I'm not much of a drinker." And then, realizing that was just what a drinker would say, I added: "It's just something that happens sometimes. I'll be all right in a minute."

Bauer was openly studying my face. I thought it was presumptuous of him, but that kind of presumption probably went with his profession, and anyway maybe I'd invited it.

"Anxiety attack?" he asked. When I didn't respond, he gave a sympathetic nod. "I know how those go. I had them for a long time. Until I found the Lord."

"Let's leave God out of this," I said.

"We can try," said Bauer. "Of course He might have something to say about that."

"Cute." I could feel Bauer's cocksure expression stirring up other old angers.

"He can help you, if you'll let Him."

"No," I said. "I've had all His help I can stand. With a friend like Him, a man doesn't need any enemies."

I expected Bauer to get angry, wanted him to. But he didn't. He looked at me the way a therapist might, his face a mask of concern, the eyes behind the mask doing some quick calculations.

"Why are you so angry at God?" he asked, after a moment. "Are you so bitter about your wife and daughter?"

For an instant I almost hit him. It was the surprise of it, the uncanny rightness of it, at a moment when I felt so vulnerable, that made his question seem like an attack. I gripped the tablecloth hard, rattling the silverware up against the plate.

"Damn you," I said. "How'd you know about that?"

Bauer blinked twice, but otherwise his expression remained unchanged. "Frank Edmundson called this evening. To see how Martha and I were doing. I asked him about you."

"You had no right to ask. And he had no right to tell you."

"Is that so?" said Bauer, giving no ground. "You mean you get to know all our secrets, but we don't get to know any of yours?"

He was right, but I was in no mood for concessions, and I didn't want to get sidetracked.

"I hate your God," I said. "I trusted Him once, and all it got me was a dead wife and baby."

"You blame God for what happened to them?"

"I did. I don't believe in God anymore. I don't believe there could be a God who lets children die. Who lets someone get to the limit of despair without helping out. I don't believe. But a religion that tries to sell a God like that as a God of love still pisses me off."

Bauer started to respond, but didn't. He ran a hand over his jaw, thinking something over. Once again he started to speak, then stopped. Finally he said: "I've caught you at a bad moment. I'm sorry if I upset you."

But I was still angry, still wanted to break through that mask. "No, you're not. There's nothing born-again Christians enjoy more than catching someone at a bad moment. So you can try to cram your religion down his throat."

Suddenly Bauer was angry. His eyes narrowed, and his hands became fists. He shifted in his chair.

"I think I'd better go," he said, starting to get up.

His anger, his retreat, broke the spell for me, and I realized that what I'd just said had been meant for someone else. I saw a flash of pain in Bauer's eyes that made me a little sick.

"Damn it, sit," I blurted, as a reflex, then softened my voice. "Please. Stay. If just for a minute."

He hesitated, and I repeated the word "please." He did sit, but on the edge of the chair, a momentary concession.

"Look, I'm sorry," I said. "I dozed off earlier, and I had a nightmare about my wife. It brought up a lot of crap. I meant what I said, but I shouldn't have thrown it at you. I'm sure you were just trying to be kind; you didn't deserve that. You're going through a terrible time right now. The last thing you need is to have your faith attacked."

Bauer settled back into his chair, but his angry look didn't change. He leaned toward me, his jaw set, pointing a finger at me like a gun.

"Don't you worry yourself about my faith, son," he said

through clenched teeth. "It's stronger than all the bitterness you got. As for trying to cram it down anyone's throat, the fact is I don't happen to believe anyone gets it that way. If I say what I believe, it's because it's precious to me and because I believe it can help others the way it's helped me. If you don't want it, that's your choice. God gave you that right." Bauer glanced at his pointing finger and folded it back into his fist. As if to compensate for the loss of one means of emphasis, his voice got louder. "Do you think I'm a simpleton? Do you think I'm blind to the horrors of this world? Do you think they don't try my faith? I've had plenty of pain in my life, plenty of reasons to hate, and I'm not just talking about what's happening now with Billy. Fourteen years ago, when I was just about your age, I sat on a riverbank pointing a gun at my head. I didn't have a single reason to live, and I had all the despair I needed to die. I would have pulled the trigger too, if the Lord hadn't spoken to me. He said: 'Don't do this thing. I know your pain. I love you. I gave my life for you. Don't cut yourself off from me. Give me a chance to show you that love.' " Bauer's voice suddenly caught, as his eyes reddened, but he kept on, driven by anger or some urgency. "Mister, I let Jesus into my heart that night, and everything changed. Every day of my life since then I've seen His face, heard His voice, felt His light, His peace, His presence. Laugh at me if you want to, but it's not foolishness, it's truth. I don't have the answers to a lot of questions. I don't know why the Lord let your wife and baby die. But I know there are answers, answers we shall all have one day. I know that because I know Him."

I certainly wasn't laughing at Bauer. I was transfixed, carried away by the emotion in his almost musical baritone voice, intrigued by his story in spite of, or maybe because of, its nostalgic familiarity. I was admiring the force and grit of the man, even while rejecting his final message.

I continued staring as he became silent, as he stared back at me with the intensity of an Old Testament prophet. Gradually his face relaxed.

"Do I make myself clear?" he said, the barest hint of a smile at the corners of his mouth.

"Loud and clear," I said. "In fact, I think you just converted half the dining room."

Bauer glanced quickly around. The few late-night diners and the help were staring at him, motionless, with mouths hanging comically open. Bauer's smile turned full and sheepish.

"Sorry about that, folks," he said, giving the room an embarrassed wave. "And don't worry. We won't be passing around the collection plate tonight."

There was some laughter, much of it nervous, as people turned back to their meals or tasks. Bauer turned back to me.

"I'm afraid I do get carried away," he said.

"You were very impressive." We looked at each other a moment, then I said: "Truce?"

"Okay."

"Maybe we'd better order. I'm starving. Have you eaten?"

"Yes."

"You must be thirsty anyway. Do you want a cocktail?"

Bauer looked at my glass. "Yes. Yes, I do. But I won't have one. I don't drink."

"Never?" I was thinking about the way he'd looked that afternoon.

"Not anymore. I used to drink pretty heavy. But I haven't had a drink in ten years." He hesitated, then his head dipped a little, as if he was conceding some objection he'd heard in the back of his mind. "Seven years, actually. I fell off the wagon that once. Went on a binge that almost killed me." He shook his head, giving a laugh that had no humor in it. "It's crazy how someone like me can want a drink after all this time, knowing what could happen. But I still do, especially when times get rough. Like this last week."

For a moment his face closed up and his eyes turned distant and sad, as if his mind were sinking into sorrow. But he pulled himself back and turned his attention to me.

"You feeling all right now?" he asked.

"Yes. Thanks."

"Go ahead and drink if you want to. It won't influence me."

"I think I'll pass too. I'm not really in the mood. And I've never been much of a drinker. My father was an alcoholic. I guess that scared me away from the stuff."

Bauer nodded slowly. "So was my father. It's tough on a kid having an alcoholic parent. The world never feels right to you; you keep thinking it's going to fall down around you. And you feel like there's something you've got to prove, though you never can." Bauer looked down, seemed to study the backs of his hands. "You were lucky it scared you off. Me, I just gave up and gave in. Did the same thing to my wife and kids as he'd done. I don't mean Martha and Billy. I was married before." He looked up, then looked away. "I know the Lord has forgiven me, but I still find it hard to forgive myself for what I did to them. If I could have just one thing to do over, it'd be that." His face brightened a little. "My girls seem to be doing pretty good now though."

I studied Bauer's face as he was looking away from me. I knew why he had a tendency to set me on edge. He managed to evoke for me at one and the same time memories of my father's relentless drinking and my mother's relentless faith. But now I began to see him apart from those associations.

His face was worn, pummeled, cracked, as if it had been through a hundred small wars, but there was a gentleness in it that had survived those wars, or maybe been born of them, gentleness that showed especially in the now clear blue eyes beneath the tangled white brows. I decided I liked his face.

The waitress came to take our orders. Bauer ordered blueberry pie and coffee. I ordered a steak dinner and coffee, and had the waitress take away my barely touched whisky.

Over dinner I told Bauer bits of my conversations with Mrs. Tate and Chief Wernecke, editing out all the pessimism about the boy's fate. We talked about Tourette's syndrome, but he didn't have much to add to what Mrs. Tate had told me. I asked him if he knew of anyone who'd been particularly upset or frightened by Billy's condition, and he said he didn't. When the dinner dishes had been cleared away, I said: "There's something else I need to ask you. Do you have any enemies who might want to hurt you through Billy?"

"No," said Bauer, too quickly, I thought.

"No? Are you sure?"

"I don't believe anyone I know would want to hurt a small boy," said Bauer, emphatically.

"Let me put it another way. Do you know of anyone around here who hates you?"

Bauer didn't answer. He just stared at me, his lips pressed tightly together.

"Tell me," I said.

Bauer shook his head. "She's suffered enough. She doesn't need any more trouble. And she couldn't be involved in this."

"You could be wrong. I need to know. If you don't tell me, I'll just try to find out on my own."

"You'll do what you think you should," said Bauer, pushing back his chair and starting to rise. "But I won't be the one who tells you."

$\triangledown$

Chapter 8

T HE RED TAILLIGHTS OF Bauer's car disappeared into the distance, and the world returned to black and white: to dark pavement, trees, mountains, and sky, dotted with street lamps and stars.

The air was cool and fresh. I took deep gulps of it, like a man filling a canteen at an oasis against the desert ahead.

It was past midnight, but I was in no rush to sleep, not after that dream. I walked south along the narrow, two-lane highway, passing a closed market, an empty park, and a row of bungalows, mostly dark. Through one small picture window a TV victim gestured wildly and soundlessly, like a mute trying to get help.

I went to the outskirts of town, crossed the highway, and started back. A small green and white sign welcomed me to Azalea, "Pop. 6126, El. 378."

I came to a long, wooden, windowless building with a pair of yellow-and-red lighted signs that announced "The Cattlemen's Bar" and "Live Country Music." I heard muffled percussion, then the melody of an old Merle Haggard ballad. I went inside.

The low-ceilinged room was dimly lit, bright only on the bandstand and behind the bar. To the left was a blacked-out pool table, some Formica-topped tables occupied by four or five different groups, and a dance floor where a couple were dancing as if they'd just been turned to pillars of salt. At the bar to my right sat a couple of old men rolling dice, and another man who stared disconsolately into his full whiskey glass, as if it were a well into which he'd just dropped something priceless. I went to an empty stretch at the middle of the counter, got a draft beer from the husky, balding bartender, and turned to listen to the music.

The band was four pieces: drums, bass, steel guitar, and electric guitar. The instrumentation was only fair, but the lead singer was really good, a bearded young man in jeans and a plaid cowboy shirt. His voice was both tuneful and gravelly, filtering the simple beauty of the song through the down-and-out quality of cigarettes and booze and hard times. His eyes were closed, either out of emotion or from wanting to pretend he was somewhere other than that small, half-empty bar.

> What a fool I was to think I could get by
> With only these few million tears I've cried.

I got hooked on country music as a kid in New Jersey, not because I grew up in the tradition—my parents' favorite music was Guy Lombardo—but because I loved cowboy movies and thought, at age four, that there was nothing more beautiful in this world than Gene Autry singing "Old Faithful Pal of Mine" to his horse Champion. A lot of country started getting marketed then as cowboy music, and songs like "I'm So Lonesome I Could Cry" had instant appeal for a little kid who'd spent most of his life feeling like he was about to burst into tears. Late grade school turned me to rock, and conversion to gospel. But when I first backslid out of Christianity in my late teens, there was country music waiting in the alley like a disreputable old friend. It was the flip side of gospel: the white soul for people who'd lost theirs, the lament of those without grace or hope.

Up on the bandstand, the singer announced a song of his

own, almost belligerently, as if daring anyone to object. No one did, but then no one seemed to be paying any attention. The singer stepped backward on the stage and back into himself, closing his eyes as the crying-steel intro began.

> On a road in Arizona
> 'Neath the dark'ning desert sky
> I been sittin' here for hours
> While the cars go passin' by
> I'm too tired to put my hand out
> I'm too tired to point my thumb
> Lost the sense of what I'm doin'
> Lost the pride in what I've done.
>
> This old road ain't goin' nowhere
> And it's too late to turn around
> Lord, I've traded all the good things
> For this empty road I've found.

"He's really good," I said, half to myself, half to a waitress who'd come up to the counter to unload some empty bottles and glasses. I wasn't expecting much of a response, but when I got none at all, I turned to take a look at her. It was Charlene Benton, the mother of the girl who'd tumbled from her bicycle that afternoon. Mrs. Benton was staring at me. Judging from the look on her face, I was about as welcome as the Ghost of Christmas Past.

"What do you want?" she asked, softly.

"A beer and some music." When her expression didn't change, I added: "My motel's up the road, and I just wandered over. Is there something the matter?"

She looked me over for another moment, then gave her head a quick, hard shake, as if administering a self-induced shock treatment. The result was a weak smile, slightly embarrassed.

"I'm sorry," she said. "I still get paranoid at the sight of a private detective. I've had enough of them to last a lifetime." She saw my puzzled look, then added: "My ex and his dear mother hired a bunch of them during the divorce. Trying to get Julie away from me."

"But they didn't."

"No," she said, with a touch of fierceness.

"I'm glad. How's Julie's knee?"

"Oh, it's fine. The minute the bandage was on she was back on her bike."

"I'll bet she was. I really like your daughter. She's got lots of spunk."

"Thanks," she said, grinning with a parent's pride.

I couldn't resist grinning along with her. Her red-brown hair, which had looked so charmingly absurd that afternoon, was now brushed softly to her shoulders and matched the femininity of the curves beneath her black skirt and white ruffled blouse. But there was still that face. It looked as if it had grown up under protest, as if its womanly lines were as superficial as the make-up and could be washed away to reveal a freckled, ten-year-old tomboy who liked climbing trees and skipping rocks and punching out ten-year-old boys.

Out of the corner of my eye I noticed the bartender hovering nearby, alternately appraising me and throwing protective looks at Charlene Benton. She noticed him too and made the kind of calming gesture an owner might make toward a large watchdog.

"Wayne, this is Mr. . . ." She gave me an apologetic look. "I'm afraid I've forgotten your name."

"Dave," I said to the bartender.

"Dave's a private detective who's here trying to help Reverend Bauer find his boy," she said. She hesitated, her expression poised at the edge of another apology. "Was it okay to say that?"

"Sure."

"It's too bad about that kid," said Wayne. "I hope he's all right." His tone was kind, but not hopeful.

As the band finished a song, someone at one of the back tables yelled for "Charlie" to come take their order. Watching as she left the counter, I saw some guy at a nearby table give her backside a pat as she went by. She did a quick turn, her eyes taking in the guy's face and his still-extended right hand.

"Freddie, you try that again and you're gonna be doin' everythin' left-handed. That includes playin' with yourself."

The offender—a crew-cut, middle-aged guy in brown work clothes—got a sheepish look, as his buddies laughed.

"Aw, come on, Charlie. Don't be such a spoilsport. I was just havin' fun. The last little girl worked here didn't mind a pat now and then."

"Well, I'm not Darla. There wasn't much of anythin' she minded. If that girl had everythin' stickin' out of her that she'd had stuck into her, she'd look like a damn porcupine."

The crack was made irresistible by the mock indignation on Charlie's freckled face and by the heavy down-home accent that had been either brought out by, or put on for, the confrontation. People at the near tables roared, and those outside the area started leaning in, asking what had been said.

"She's quite a character," I said to Wayne.

"She sure is," he said, smiling and shaking his head with a kind of bewildered affection. "She sure in hell is."

For a few minutes Wayne got busy filling orders for Charlie and for the customers sitting at the bar. Then he came back to where I was sitting, leaning his arms against the counter.

"I hope you can do the Bauers some good," he said.

"So do I. You know them?"

"Not really. I'm not much on religion myself. I do see the Reverend around town some. We joke around a bit. A lot of them fundamentalists look at a bar guy like me like he's somethin' the cat drug in. But not him. He's an okay guy. I feel real sorry for him. What a shitty thing to happen."

Wayne was silent for a moment, then asked: "You been in town long?" When I shook my head, he said: "Folks here are pretty upset about the whole thing. You hear about stuff like that all the time on the television, but no one figured it could happen here. Not in a town like this one. Out where we are." His mouth bunched up in disgust, and his eyes grew reflective. "It's gettin' so no place is safe anymore. World's goin' to hell in a fuckin' handbasket. I guess it's no wonder when those bleeding heart judges are letting . . ."

I nodded politely, tuning out the too familiar tirade until it was merely white noise. Into focus came the singer's voice doing Haggard's "Are the Good Times Really Over?" which wasn't much more to my liking, but at least it had a melody. But then some of the bartender's words started breaking through again, and suddenly what he was saying took on a different meaning.

"Wait a minute, Wayne," I said. "Are you talking about a particular guy?"

"Tuttle," he said, spitting out the name. "The fucking pervert."

"Who?" I asked, trying to hide my feeling of surprise.

"Henry Tuttle. You ain't never heard about him?"

I shook my head.

"Well, he's a son-of-a-bitchin' child molester, and he's walkin' around this town free as a fuckin' bird. Jesus. If I was those cops I'd have him in a back room strung up by the balls until he told me what he did with that boy." For a moment Wayne considered that image with an expression of grim satisfaction. Then he gave a sigh. "Guess it's not fair to blame the cops. I talked with a guy I know on the force. He says they checked out Tuttle and couldn't get anything on him. He says they're watchin' him pretty close, but that's all they can do. Their hands are pretty well tied. Jesus, if we'd just give the cops the power to—"

The bartender was launching into another tirade, and I put up a hand to stop him. "Tell me about Tuttle."

Wayne looked a little disappointed by the interruption, but warmed to the more specific subject at once.

"Used to be a maintenance guy at a grade school down in Carlyle. That's south of here, near Porterville. They caught him diddling some of the students. Seven-year-olds, I think. Girls and boys." His look of distaste deepened as he said the word "boys." "It was quite a scandal around here. Made all the papers. I'm surprised you didn't read about it in . . . where you from?"

"The Bay Area."

Wayne's eyes narrowed as if I'd just divulged some dirty secret. "Maybe it didn't get that far. Or maybe nobody noticed with all the crap that goes on up there." He gave me a wary look, as if the Bay Area were some kind of infectious disease.

"What happened to Tuttle?"

"He went to jail for a year. Can you believe it? One fuckin' year. They should of hung him."

"What's he doing here?"

Wayne's face got a sick look. "He was raised here. His mother lives here. Bunch of people would of liked to run him out of town, but the cops put a stop to that fast. They gotta uphold the law, and the law's there to protect the guilty, right? Then, on top of that, those bastards at the phone company went and gave that pervert a good job as a technician. Jesus. Guess we all know now what they mean by 'reach out and touch someone.' " Wayne didn't bother to smile at his own bitter joke.

Charlie came back to the bar with a tray full of ashes and empties, and gave Wayne another order. In the background the band was playing something fast and tuneless with a heavy bass run—obviously a break song.

"So. You like the band or what?" she asked.

"I like them. Especially the singer."

"Jim's real popular around here," said Charlie, in a tone that was matter-of-fact rather than enthusiastic. "You wouldn't know it from the size of the crowd tonight—but Thursday's dead everywhere. Come tomorrow night this place'll be jammed with people. From all over the county. Lots of people say Jim should try his luck in Nashville. I know he's dying to, but he's a little short of cash." She laughed. "Havin' two ex-wives and three kids to support kinda puts a crimp in your style."

Over her shoulder I saw the band members leaving the small stage, each heading to a separate section of the room, getting a break from each other as well as from the music. The singer headed our way. He called to Wayne for a beer, then looked at Charlie.

"Hey, sweet thing, you still savin' yourself for ole Jim?"

"Dream on," said Charlie.

The singer glanced at me, then did a double take, recognizing me a few seconds after I'd recognized him.

"You're the guy from the church," he said, puzzled.

"And you're the guy who likes to go around shocking the Christians."

He laughed. "It's a dirty job but someone's gotta do it. Anyway, they love it. Brings a little excitement into their dreary lives. And lets them feel self-righteous as hell."

He took a Budweiser from the bartender, then lifted a shot glass of whiskey off Charlie's full tray, as if he were a cocktail party guest being invited to help himself. She started to protest, then just shook her head. The bartender added a full shot glass to the tray, without annoyance, saying he'd put in on the singer's tab.

"Since you're in here, I guess you ain't one of them," said the singer to me. "What were you doing at Azalea Bible?"

"Some business."

"What were *you* doing there, Jim?" said Charlie. "Stealin' from the collection plate?"

"I was lookin' for my old man. He's a bigwig over there. Fits in real well too. He's a hypocrite, just like the rest of them."

"They're not all like that," said Charlie.

"Bullshit."

"Not Reverend Bauer," she said. "I know him. He's nice."

The singer—I remembered now that Mrs. Seifert had said his name was Jim Hadley—got a gleam in his eye. "Bauer's kind of nice—I'll give you that. But when it comes to hypocrites, lady, he's the Chief Pharisee."

Charlie threw Hadley a disgusted look.

"Oh yeah," he said, in response. "Well, what would you say if I told you old man Bauer's been shackin' up with that woman that runs the day-care center?"

"I'd say you're full of it."

"Yea, well, just ask Arnie if you don't believe me. He

saw 'em coming out of a motel down in Porterville. What do you think they were doin' there, huh? A little religious counseling?"

"I think Arnie's a liar."

Charlie picked up her tray and headed off toward the tables. Hadley watched her go, then turned to me, started to say something, shrugged, and moved down the bar. A couple of women who had arrived a short time ago greeted Hadley with adoring expressions. He cracked a joke to one of them, a busty brunette, who laughed and put a hand over the top of her low-cut blouse in mock modesty.

"I don't believe him," said Charlie, as she came back to the bar a few moments later. "He's got a real nasty streak, and he'll say anything." She looked up at me. "You ran into Jim before?"

"Literally. He didn't strike me as a real pleasant guy."

"Sweet songs and a sour puss—that's what one of his exes says about him." Charlie was silent for a moment, thinking. "Anyway, if he's right, I wouldn't blame him."

"What was that?" I asked, confused by her syntax.

"Sorry. I meant I wouldn't blame Reverend Bauer if Jim's right about him and Mrs. Tate. Not that I think he is right. But I like Elizabeth Tate a lot. She took care of Julie for a while and was real good to her. She's a sweet woman. Not like Mrs. Bauer."

I remembered that look of distaste on Mrs. Bauer's face when she'd mentioned that Charlie was a cocktail waitress. Apparently she hadn't hidden that distaste from Charlie. As if Charlie were confronting it now and feeling defensive, she said: "I won't be doing this much longer. I been taking some business classes part-time at Sequoia. Mostly bookkeeping. I get my A.A. in December. Then I can get myself a decent job."

"Good for you."

"Not that I think there's anything wrong with working here. And some of the people are real nice. But I want better things for Julie and me. And sometimes I get real tired of this place."

Charlie glanced around the dark, smoke-filled bar. The

jukebox slid from "Honky Tonk Heaven" to "If You've Got Ten Minutes, Let's Fall in Love." Suddenly the jukebox was cut off in mid-melody, as if some higher authority had also gotten tired of the scene.

The band members were heading back to the stage for what had to be their last set. Or three of them were. They seemed to have lost the fourth.

"Arnie, where's Truckee?" said Hadley, looking around.

"I don't know," said a stocky young man, the drummer. "Last time I saw him he was heading out back with some broad."

"Well, go roust his sorry ass out of whatever backseat he's in and tell him to get the hell in here."

I took the last few swallows of my beer, watched Charlie as she moved off among the tables, and tried to decide if I wanted to leave. Suddenly a voice at the back of the bar was screaming for someone to call an ambulance, that Truckee had been hurt. I saw Wayne pick up the phone, and I followed the others outside.

The back of the bar was a dirty parking lot, with a few sprinkles of gravel, full of drainage ruts that hadn't been repaired since the winter rains. From the back of the building hung a single floodlight, which cast a sickly yellow glow over the parking area and the shadowy, tall-weeded lot beyond.

Truckee, a lanky, beardless redhead, wearing jeans and a blue work shirt, was lying on his back in the dirt. One knee was raised, as if clenched in pain; the other leg was lying inert, the lower part of it jutting out at an unnatural angle that could only mean a bad fracture. The back of one forearm was laid like a compress across his forehead; below it, his nose and mouth were bleeding. He was half moaning, half crying.

Hadley was kneeling next to him, touching his chest, moaning with him. "Oh shit, Truckee. Oh shit, man."

"The bastards. They busted my leg, Jimmy. Oh God, they busted my leg. It hurts so bad."

"Hush now," said Hadley. "Don't try to talk. There's an

ambulance coming. You're gonna be okay. It won't hurt much longer."

"Watch it, Jimmy. They said . . ."

"Don't talk," said Hadley, and this time his words sounded like an order.

Truckee glanced around at the small crowd then, as if seeing us for the first time. He nodded, bit down on his lip, and resumed his moaning. A siren sounded in the distance.

$\triangledown$

Chapter 9

THE AMBULANCE WAS GONE, and the black-and-white, and the cars of the bar patrons. The three remaining band members were filing back into the bar in postures of exhaustion, as if that last hour in the parking lot had been eight hours of hard labor.

Feet shifted on the gravel nearby, and I noticed Charlie. A short time ago she'd been the model of competence, wiping Truckee's face with cold towels and helping comfort him until the ambulance arrived. Now the competence had given way to a look of misery.

"You okay?" I asked.

"I guess. But I can't stop thinking of the way his leg looked. It was terrible. And to think they did that to him on purpose."

The story the cops had gotten was that a woman had lured Truckee outside where two men had knocked him down and broken his leg with a tire iron. Truckee had denied knowing any of the three or why it had happened. A couple of people had gotten a look at the young blond woman who'd entered the back door of the bar just after the band had taken their break, but they said they'd never seen her before.

"You have any ideas about that?" I asked, gesturing toward the place where Truckee had lain, a place marked by scuffed dirt and a few splotches of blood.

64

Charlie shrugged, glancing over her shoulder at where the band members had been a few moments before. "I heard some things. I don't know if they're true."

"What things?"

"That Truckee borrowed money from some bad people and was having trouble paying it back."

"You didn't tell the police that. No one did."

Her head made a slight ducking motion. "If Truckee doesn't want 'em to know, why should I tell 'em? I don't want to make things worse for him. Anyway, I'm not sure it's true."

She continued to stare at the blood-smeared dirt, then hugged herself, as if cold. The gesture made her seem momentarily childlike. Some reflex made me start to put my arm around her until sense told me it wasn't my place.

"I was thinking of getting a cup of coffee if there's some place still open," I said. "Can I buy you a cup?"

Her body stiffened at the invitation. "No. I got to get home."

"Okay."

Her body relaxed as if it had been freed from some pressure. She looked at me a moment, then said, "Sorry. I didn't mean to be rude. It's been an awful night."

"I know."

"I guess I could use a cup if we make it quick. And if you don't mind waiting while I finish up inside. We'll need two cars. Where's yours?"

"At the motel. I'll get it."

Fifteen minutes later I followed her blue Ford station wagon to a Perko's coffee shop just outside of town on a small highway that ran between Route 99 and the Sierras. The interior of Perko's had that timeless, scrubbed look of so many twenty-four-hour restaurants, and only the customers signalled the lateness of the hour: two bleary-eyed truckers joking with a waitress; a young man dozing in a booth with his head against a knapsack; a group of sobering partygoers straining for laughs.

We took a booth near the back and let the waitress pour

us cups of coffee. Charlie took a sip of hers, then put her cup down. Her eyes got a faraway look.

"That was terrible," she said.

"The coffee?" I asked, purposely misunderstanding her.

"No," she said, starting to laugh. *"Tonight."*

Her laugh was all out of proportion to the lame joke, one of those senseless late-night laughs, born of nerves perhaps in this case, but hearty, not nervous sounding. She turned her grin toward me for a moment, as if it was something she owed me a share of. I was glad to take it.

I could feel my attitude toward Charlie changing. I had maybe fifteen years on this woman. At first I'd looked at her the way a man might look at a high school girl, conscious of a sexual attraction but trying to defuse it either by adopting a paternalistic stance or by passing it off to a younger self, remembering when one was that age. But that strategy didn't seem to be working very well. I now found myself thinking things like: She isn't as young as she looks; she's been married, she has a seven-year-old daughter, she's not a child; fifteen years isn't all that much. As I looked at the red-brown hair, the beautiful green eyes, those freckles, that grin, and the soft curves of her breasts under the silky blouse, I kept thinking: This woman's an absolute doll.

There came a moment when we both seemed to realize that we had been studying each other. Charlie's eyes flickered with a touch of embarrassment, then she recovered herself.

"You like being a detective?" she asked.

"Yeah. Some of it."

"What do you like best about it?"

"That's hard. Sometimes there's excitement, but usually not. Sometimes justice gets done, but more often the results are ambiguous. Sometimes the people are interesting, but often they're just sad. Maybe it's the figuring things out that I like best. Going into some situation where nothing's clear and making some sense of it."

"What kinds of cases do you handle?"

"Different kinds. The last one was tracking down a runaway. The one before that involved drug dealing in an auto plant. The one before that one was a possible murder case."

"That sounds exciting."

"It wasn't, as it turned out. A couple came to me whose daughter had died. The D.A. had decided it was a suicide. The couple thought the son-in-law had murdered her. They hired me to collect evidence against him. But after I looked into it for a while I became morally certain that the D.A. was right, that the parents just didn't want to see the truth. They ignored what I told them and hired another investigator. So it was just a waste of my time and their money. At least it will be a waste of their money if I ever get them to pay what they owe me."

"They wouldn't pay you, huh?"

"No. They said I was incompetent, that I was in league with the district attorney, and lots more. I guess I can sympathize. They're old-world Catholics, and the idea of a daughter's suicide got them pretty upset. But I still want my money."

"You handle divorce cases?"

"There aren't many of those with no-fault divorce."

"I guess I mean custody cases." Charlie said the words with a slight smile, knowing I knew what answer she had to want. But there was no smile in her eyes.

"I've helped track down a parent or two who acted against a court order by trying to hide the children from the other parent. But I don't gather evidence for one parent against another. I have a good friend, a therapist, who specializes in custody mediation. She's indoctrinated me pretty heavily on that stuff—if I ever needed it."

Charlie visibly relaxed. "I wish all detectives felt like you. Might have saved me a lot of grief."

"You had a pretty rough time of it, huh?"

"Yeah."

"Was it the usual thing? Your ex trying to get back at you for the divorce through your daughter?"

"It wasn't Chad. My ex. It was his mother. Chad never paid that much attention to Julie when we were together.

Fact is, Chad never paid that much attention to anything but Chad." Charlie gave a little grin, then made a slight hissing sound to show that she knew she was being catty. "It was all his mother's doing. She owns a ranch up in Gilroy. She's a tough woman. Loaded with money. Chad's her only son. Maybe she was worried that Julie would be her only grandchild. When I kicked her precious son out of the house, she decided she wanted her granddaughter with her. She thinks she can do anything better than anyone else, including raising children. Though she couldn't prove it through Chad far as I'm concerned." Another glimmer of that grin. "Plus she never liked me very much. She thinks Chad married beneath him. And I never took any crap from her. So she went after Julie—with the best lawyers she could buy. And those detectives."

"You won, though."

"Yeah. Barely. I went a little wild after Chad and I separated. Nothing real bad, but they brought up all of that. They made a big deal out of my working in the bar. And they made up a bunch of stuff. All I had was me and some young lawyer from town who'd just passed his bar exam. Nice guy, but not real sharp. It sure was close."

She made a little "whew" sound and brushed the back of her hand across her forehead, as if she were a laborer just finishing a day of trenching. The gesture was especially comic against the backdrop of her brushed hair and make-up.

"I'm glad it turned out all right."

"It will, anyway. Once I get my degree. It's been kind of rough, though. Chad's just been hanging around his mother's place, letting her support him, getting out of paying much child support. While his mother's been offering me money to give up Julie. The bitch. We've just been scraping by. But that's gonna change." She paused, then smiled. "But enough of my hard-luck stories. What about yours?" There was a subtle change in her eyes, a hesitancy. "Or maybe you don't have any. Maybe you're happily married."

"I'm not married anymore."

"Any kids?"

"No."

I was going to leave it at that, as I usually did, but this time silence felt like some kind of betrayal, though of what or of whom I couldn't say.

"I did have one child," I said. "A little girl. She died of crib death."

Charlie gave a small moan. She made a gesture as if to touch my hand, but stopped, letting her hand drop at the middle of the table. "That's terrible. The same thing happened to a cousin of mine. It tore her up something awful. But she already had two kids. I think that's what got her through. Must be much worse when it's your only one. For both of you, but especially your wife."

I nodded, swallowing hard. That still-vivid grief started welling up, and I could feel my insides close around it like a steel casing.

"I'd think something like that would either bring two people real close together or pull them apart," said Charlie. "Did it . . . ? I mean, was that what . . . ?"

I nodded again. "She couldn't handle it. She . . ."

My voice, which sounded strange to my ears, just seemed to give out. It was still so hard to talk about Katie, even after two years. Not the baby, just Katie. There had been such a difference in those two deaths for me. It had hurt like hell when the baby had died, but the mourning had been over soon enough. Fatherhood for me had been something too new, almost theoretical. Pregnancy, after those first absurd congratulations, had been Katie's time, to pamper her, to try to understand her absorption, to stifle the irritations I often felt at the disruption of our old life, to leave her and the women to the mysteries they shared together. I'd always liked little kids—maybe the consequence of having a younger sister—but babies were something else to me: fragile, not-quite-human creatures to be loved for what they would soon be. I'd come to have real feelings of paternity by the time the baby died, but they were nothing compared to what Katie must have felt, Katie who'd carried her, who'd done most of the caretaking, who had a natural love for babies in a way

I'd never had. But if I understood something of the difference in our feelings, I still couldn't understand Katie's bottomless despair, her refusal to survive.

Katie: my beautiful, fragile, dreamy woman. I'd been drawn to her almost ethereal beauty, had felt the desire to protect her from the consequences of her own delicacy. But more than anything else, there had been some fundamental need, even desperation, in me to try to reach across the distances I sensed in her, to get close to her—as if by doing so I could span some distances inside myself and heal some ancient wound. I'd felt I'd almost made it before her pregnancy, but then she seemed to pull back, as if she'd taken what was most essential to her in our relationship and didn't need me as much anymore. And after the baby died, she just wandered away into those always melancholy, now despondent, vistas inside herself, while I watched her recede far past the point where she could hear me, or I her, until she disappeared.

I remembered the dream that Mrs. Tate had told me, of reaching out to Billy, who wouldn't reach back. I'd dreamed of Katie in that way so many times. Whether the medium was dark water, or dark chasm, or just darkness, what happened was always the same: I couldn't quite get to her and she wouldn't do the little she had to do to help me save her. My feelings in the dream ran the gamut of fear, sorrow, helplessness, and hopelessness, but the feeling that ended it and began the waking was always the same: rage that she hadn't loved me enough to live. That rage was in me still.

"Are you okay?" I heard Charlie saying, as if from a distance.

Her face came into focus, full of worry. Somehow her expression filled me with alarm, like the face of an onlooker as you wake from an accident, whose sympathy tells you that something is very wrong. I wanted to get up, to move, to prove I was all right.

"It's late," I said, gruffly. "We'd better go."

I put a couple of dollars down on the table top, snapping at Charlie when she tried to pay her share. I stood and waited formally as she stood, then walked so fast she had to scurry to keep up. Movement and then the rush of cool air as we got outside took the edge off my panic, but my one desire was still to get away from there, to be alone.

"Hey, you okay?" asked Charlie, just behind me. "What is it?"

"I'm fine," I said, an edge of anger in my voice. "It's something that happens sometimes. I'll be okay. I just need to get back to the motel."

"You sure you can drive?"

"Yes."

I got out my car keys, fumbled for the right one, got the door open, then stopped.

When I first started getting those panic attacks after Katie's death, or at least when I first knew what they were and how I'd have to face up to them if they weren't to take control of me, the words "I don't run anymore" had become my private anthem against retreat. The words came to me now, along with the realization that I had a special reason for not wanting to run this time. I turned and faced Charlie.

"My wife's dead," I said, quickly, in a voice so tightly controlled it was toneless, with maybe only a slight tremor. "She killed herself two years ago, a year after the baby died."

As I spoke I watched Charlie carefully, pessimistically, waiting for one of the reactions I didn't want: some panic of her own; an I-don't-need-this-shit turning away; an it-was-my-fault-for-bringing-it-up taking of responsibility; a profusion of overdone condolences. She showed none of them.

"That's so sad," she said softly, her eyes fixed on mine. "How terrible for you."

We stared at each other for a few moments. Then I said: "I'd better go. I'm sorry the evening got broken up. I enjoyed what little there was of it."

"Me too."

"I need to talk to you and Julie about Billy. Could I come by tomorrow? Maybe in the morning?"

I realized as I spoke that there was something else I was trying to say. But it just wasn't my night for saying things. Still, maybe she caught it after all. She said: "I promised Julie some waffles tomorrow. We'll be eating around ten-thirty. You're welcome if you'd like to come by."

"I'll be there."

She smiled. "Good."

I got in my car, waited until I knew Charlie's car had started, then drove off. I rolled down the window to let in the cool air and flicked on the radio to KNGS, wanting to fill my head with noise. There was a Ricky Scaggs song, a Con Hunley, a Willie Nelson, then one other. As the last song started, I felt a quick intake of breath, felt my hand rush for the dial. I pulled back my hand.

Katie had hated country music, though she'd humored me about it, but there'd been a few songs she'd liked, including this old Bobby Bare tune that had come as close to an "our song" as any we'd had. I'd switched it off maybe ten times since Katie's death, feeling with the familiar opening chords a surge of tears I didn't want. Tonight I left it on and let them come.

A day like all the rest I've struggled through
Changed into this magic time with you
Once again my hands and eyes take your beauty in
Just in case a night like this one never comes again.

Chapter 10

It WAS ONLY 9:00 A.M., but the freshness of morning was gone. The humid heat had moved in like a mild depression, dampening the spirit, adding a heaviness to things.

The street of tract houses was empty of life. Only the fan-shaped sprinklers moved, back and forth, like ineffectual hands trying to wave back the heat.

I walked along the sidewalk checking mailbox numbers until I found the number I wanted. A couple of houses away two children emerged with their toys. They stopped when they saw me, staring open-mouthed. Maybe all the children around here had been given a quick course in fear since the Bauer boy's disappearance. Or maybe it had to do with the house I was going to.

Not that the house itself looked in any way disreputable. The beige paint was fairly fresh, the lawn mowed, the low juniper hedge along the sidewalk trimmed, the jasmine along the walkway carefully tended. If it stood out at all it was for being a little better kept than the other clones in this tract.

I went up the front steps and rang the bell. There was a slight parting of the curtain drawn across the picture window, as someone took a surreptitious look at me. The look didn't bring anyone to the door, so I leaned on the bell. Eventually the front door opened with a soft whooshing sound that resembled an exasperated sigh.

Henry Tuttle appeared behind the screen door, wearing a maroon bathrobe over blue pajamas. His hair was uncombed, sticking up in wisps around his balding forehead. He hadn't shaved, and the mesh of the screen door exaggerated the darkness of his day-old beard. There was a fresh bandage on his right cheek.

"Hi," he said, without tone in his voice. A thin smile acknowledged some minimum obligation of friendliness, while his wary eyes looked for some sign of threat.

"How're you feeling?"

"Okay. They put a couple of stitches in my cheek. The rest was just bruises. I felt pretty shaky last night. Today I'm better."

"That's good."

We stared at each other a moment. Tuttle shifted restlessly from one foot to the other, obviously hoping I would go away. When I didn't, he asked: "How'd you find me?"

"I looked for you at work. They told me you stayed home today."

Tuttle squinted. "How'd you know where I worked?"

"Someone mentioned it."

"Chief Wernecke?"

"No. He wouldn't say much about you. I overheard someone else talking about you."

Tuttle's eyes closed and his shoulders slumped, as against the weight of some inevitable burden.

"I'm sure they said only good things," he said, with a kind of hopeless sarcasm.

"Not such good things, actually."

"So then what? You're sorry now you helped me out? Maybe you're here to do what you stopped those boys from doing."

"Don't get paranoid. I'm not sorry I helped you. And I'm not here to hurt you."

" 'Don't get paranoid,' the man says. Even paranoids have real enemies, don't you know? I got a town full of them."

"Then why'd you come here? Why didn't you go some-where where no one knew about you?"

Tuttle shrugged. "Because I was broke and needed some-place to stay. Because I got a mother who's willing to take me in, and because I need to have someone who still gives a damn about me. And because I figured that wherever I went, the word would get around somehow. My therapist said I'd have to face people sometime. Easy for him to say."

"Maybe people will forget in time."

Tuttle gave a slow, firm shake of his head, his face stern, like a judge denying a defendant's petition for mercy. "They're never going to forget. Never." Then he shifted back from judge to judged, giving me a wary look. "So what'd you want with me?"

"I'm a private detective hired to find out what I can about Billy Bauer. I'd like to talk to you about that."

"Oh, shit." Tuttle's eyes closed for a moment, and a look of exhaustion came over his face. "And you're the one telling me not to be paranoid. Something happens to some kid, the first person everyone looks at is me."

"Can you blame them?"

"I don't have the right to blame them," said Tuttle, his voice full of self-pity. "Perverts like me don't have any rights at all. Anybody can do anything they want to me."

"You know that's not true."

"Oh, yeah," said Tuttle, challenging me.

"You've got the right to press charges against those boys. I talked to Wernecke about it yesterday. He wasn't pleased about the way Dawson handled the thing. He wants you to know that the police will cooperate with you if you want to press charges."

"No kidding?" For a moment Tuttle looked pleased. Then hopelessness began to seep back into his face, fitting its contours like new leakage to an old stain. "It wouldn't do me any good. I'd just end up paying more than they would. People around here would see to that. Anyway, I've had enough of the police. Soon as the boy went missing, they came down on me. They went over this place and me like they were going through a garbage can. Holding their noses the whole time. I know what the police think of me." For a moment Tuttle was silent, glum. Then his face brightened a little, in a belligerent sort of way. "They didn't find anything though, because there's nothing to find. Ask them."

"The police aren't telling me much about the Bauer case. I'd rather you talk to me yourself."

"I don't want to talk about it anymore." Tuttle took a step back, gripping the edge of the front door. "I don't have to talk to you, do I?"

"No. You don't."

"All right then." But he hesitated. "Would you, if you were me?"

"It depends. If I had something to hide, I'd slam the door right now. If I didn't, I think I'd talk. It might help you some with the people around here if you openly cooperated in this. It would certainly help you if this case got cleared up."

Tuttle bit at his lip. He glanced from me to the hand he had resting on the door. Finally he dropped the hand, like a fighter dropping his guard. He reached forward to unlatch the screen.

"I guess you might as well come in," he said.

The living-room furnishings looked like those of an elderly woman: an overstuffed couch with lacy throw pillows, several straight-backed chairs with needlepoint seat covers, and dozens of old family photographs on top of the sideboard and the large television set. Tuttle took a seat on one end of the couch, wrapping his robe tightly around him, as if it would offer him some kind of protection. I sat on the opposite end.

"My mother will be back in an hour or so," said Tuttle. "I want to get this over before she gets back."

"All right. Maybe it would speed things up if you just told me what you told the police."

"I told them I didn't have anything to do with what happened to that boy," said Tuttle quickly, almost fiercely. "And it's true. I didn't."

Tuttle stared at me, his eyes challenging me to challenge him. I just waited. After a time he dropped his eyes.

"I did know the boy, though," he said. "Not well, but I knew him."

"How?"

"We met at the shrink's office."

"You're seeing Dr. Rodenbaugh?"

Tuttle shook his head. "Dr. Tishman. They're partners. Billy and I had the same appointment time. For a while anyway. He usually came with his father. Though once he came with his mother. And another time with a woman he called Elizabeth."

"Elizabeth Tate. She runs the day-care center."

Tuttle nodded, with only mild interest. "He was a nice kid. Shy. Sort of sad-looking. But friendly once he got to know you. And kind. A lot of kids aren't, but he was." Tuttle smiled at the thought. "Sometimes we'd see each other for just a couple of minutes. Other times we'd both be there early. Billy and I got to talking, made friends. I'd tell him a story, or we'd play cards. It got so he'd bring things to show me, like a picture he'd done or a toy he'd gotten. It was real nice."

Tuttle paused, remembering, and his face took on a look of pure happiness. But after a moment his eyes shifted to me, and he looked startled and shamed, as if he'd been observed in some very private act. He looked away, then seemed to compose himself.

"His father didn't know who I was then, so he didn't know he was supposed to be afraid of me. He was kind of nervous of me at first—I guess you always wonder why someone else is seeing a shrink—but after a while he began to relax. It was somethin' being around a kid again. It was the first time since . . . that other stuff happened. Maybe it's the last too."

Tuttle glanced down, his hands gripping his robe into tight wrinkles. His forehead wrinkled too, like something attached to the garment.

"Did you know what was wrong with Billy?" I asked.

"Not at first," said Tuttle. His gaze drifted off, searching out a memory. "But one day Billy's father got called in to talk to the doctor without Billy. That happened sometimes.

But this time the receptionist got called out for something too. There weren't any other patients there. It was the only time since I been out that I been alone with a kid. The court says I'm never supposed to be. I figured it must be all right there in the doctor's office. And it wasn't my doing. But I got frightened, I couldn't help it. Not just about getting into trouble. I got scared of what I might do. That didn't make any sense—not really—I never been out of control, even before. But when everybody tells you you're horrible, it makes you doubt yourself. I tried to look calm—I didn't want to scare the kid—but maybe he picked up on what I was feeling. That's what the doctors figured later, when we talked about it. I never touched him—I even moved away. But suddenly *he* went out of control, screaming all these horrible things. Everybody rushed into the room. God, I've never been so frightened in all my life. Never."

Tuttle's eyes were wide, mesmerized by the memory. Then he seemed to jerk himself loose with a quick shake of the shoulders.

"It turned out all right, though," he said. "Here I thought everyone was gonna come down on me, and instead they were all asking me if *I* was all right. I couldn't believe it. That's when they told me what was wrong with Billy. I think the father expected me to be angry. He couldn't know I was too relieved to think about being angry. He seemed grateful I wasn't. That was sure something: me being the nice guy for a change."

"When did you see Billy last?"

"About a week and a half ago. In town. He was with his father. He waved. I waved back."

"Did you speak to him?"

"No. His father knew about me by then. I wouldn't have dared."

"When did he find out?"

"About a month ago. I ran into them in a grocery store here. I'd seen them in Azalea a few times—from a distance. But I never let them see me here 'cause I didn't want them to find out who I was. I never gave them my last name at the shrink's office. Anyway that day I was in the grocery store, people looking at me and whispering like they always do, and all of a sudden I heard this little voice say, "Hi, Henry," and Billy came running up and gave me a hug. It was awful—like in a movie theater when something goes wrong with the projector and the movie just stops, you know, with a picture just frozen up there on the screen. Everything stopped moving. The whole store was quiet. Except for Billy and his father. Reverend Bauer was real friendly, but I knew he'd be finding out about me real fast. We talked for a little bit—I can't remember what I said—then he headed for the checkout counter with his groceries. I ducked down one of the aisles where I could see them without them seeing me. People at the checkout counter were yapping at him a mile a minute, and he kept frowning, glancing back around the store. Next time I went to the psychiatrist's office, Billy wasn't there. When I asked about it, the receptionist told me that Billy's appointment time had been changed. She said there was a scheduling conflict. I'm sure." Tuttle's shoulders twitched up and down. "I knew it had to happen eventually. But it was nice for a while, having a friend again."

Tuttle looked down. For a moment his face held a childlike look of misery: brow furrowed, mouth tight, cheeks and lips puffed as if barely holding back a cry.

"The police must have asked you what you were doing at the time Billy disappeared."

As Tuttle looked up, the misery in his face aged thirty years.

"If you're asking me if I have an alibi for that evening, well, I don't. That day I got off work at four and drove into the mountains. By myself. I do that a lot—just to get away from things. I came home about eight-thirty."

"What car?"

"My mother's station wagon. Chevy Cavalier. We share it. She doesn't need it much. No one around town wants to give me any credit. Makes it kind of hard to buy on your own." He paused, thinking something over. Whatever it was began spilling bitterness into his face. "They're never through making you pay, are they? You serve your time, you get your therapy, and you think you've paid your debt, but you never have. Never. Not for what I've done. Touch a child and everyone in the world thinks they're better than you. Even the con who rapes old ladies and slits their throats thinks he's better than you—looks at you like a hellfire preacher—and thinks he should slit your throat. If they'd sent me someplace really hard, I'd be dead by now. Even where I was I had a couple of close calls. There were so many times I was afraid I'd never get out of there alive. Now, sometimes, I wish I hadn't."

Tuttle sat very still, his whole body cramped inward, staring desolately into his private hell. As if making a last-ditch appeal for mercy, he said: "I'd never hurt a child. Oh, I know they say that what I did hurt those kids, but I don't see . . . I never hit them or anything. I never had sex with them. I don't like sex. They were my friends, that's all. We used to play together, talk about things. Sure I touched them places, but it's all right to touch your friends, isn't it? It was just silly games we were playing. It didn't feel dirty. Not until those people found us. The way they looked at me. God. It was them that had the dirty minds. It was them that scared the kids, made them feel like it was dirty."

Tuttle's head was lowered as he spoke. He started to look up at me, then didn't. "Oh, I know it was wrong," he said quickly, as if knowing without looking the objection he'd find on my face, on anyone's face. "But it's hard for me to . . ." He paused, trying to sort out his thoughts. "I love kids. I'm happy when I'm with them. I don't feel that way with grownups. With grownups I just feel lonely. My shrink says I still feel like a child inside and I got to grow up. But something's missing in me; I don't know how. I'd give anything to be with kids again. I'd promise never to touch them again. I wouldn't, really I wouldn't. Do you think that's so much to ask? But they'll never let me. God damn it, they'll never let me."

Tuttle became silent. He was sitting on the edge of the couch, bent forward, arms crossed over his stomach. When

I asked him if he was all right, he nodded. When I told him I was leaving, he nodded again.

Outside I got in my car, drove half a block, U-turned at a cul-de-sac, and started back the way I'd come. As I passed Tuttle's house, I saw him standing at the picture window, framed by the slightly open drapes, staring at the children playing down the street. Behind that glass, wearing pajamas and robe, he reminded me of a hospital patient in one of those plastic bubbles, isolated because of some rare infectious disease, looking out at a world he could never touch again.

▽

Chapter 11

IT WAS JULIE WHO answered the bell, appearing behind the screen door, moving stiff-legged with her silver brace. She was wearing another shorts outfit, this one red, with a matching ribbon at the base of her ponytail.

"Hi," she said, cheerily. "You're late."

"Jul-ie," scolded her mother from the back of the house.

"I'm not that late, am I?" I said, checking my watch. "Anyway, I thought your Mom might like a little extra time to get things ready."

"Mom's been up since seven," said the girl. "She's real twitchy today. She acts like you're . . ."

"Julie!"

Julie grinned at her mischief, as her mother came racing up behind her, embarrassed. Charlie gave Julie a strained, "Now, sweetheart, be good," as she moved her aside and pushed open the screen door.

"I hope I didn't hold things up," I said.

"No, no," said Charlie, while her daughter gave a comic's roll of the eyes behind her. "Come on in."

Charlie's red hair was pulled up at the back of her head, with a few wisps lying along her neck. She was wearing an aqua sundress that flattered her figure and brought out the color in her eyes. There was some extra sparkle in those eyes, perhaps the vestiges of embarrassment, that made them look especially beautiful.

"You look great," I said,

"Thanks," she said, obviously pleased. "I'm glad you're here."

"I am too."

We stared at each other a moment, smiling foolishly. To the side and below, Julie observed these male-female goings-on in the detached, skeptical way that young kids do, that makes them seem in this one context older and wiser beings. We both glanced at Julie as if asking some tolerance. Her response was to blow a large gum bubble, then snap it.

"So . . ." said Charlie, uncomfortably. "You hungry or what?"

"I'm hungry."

"Good. I'm gonna need a few more minutes to get things ready. Julie, why don't you show Dave to the living room."

"Mother," said Julie, with what sounded like infinite weariness, "I think he can find the living room himself. We're in it."

Which, in a way, we were. This house was too minuscule for extras like an entrance hall. The front portion was divided into living room and dining room by furniture, not partitions, and whether or not we were now in the living room was a question only a sophist would tackle.

"Julie, don't be difficult," said Charlie, trying at once to soften the remark for me with a smile and toughen it for her daughter with an eye signal I wasn't supposed to catch. "I'd like you to keep Dave company for a minute."

Charlie gave her daughter a last look of appeal or threat, then went off toward the kitchen, calling back to me: "Please don't mind the place—we're sort of camping out until I finish school."

The living-room furnishings were basically garage-sale stuff, but selected with a nice eye for color: rust and green and beige to go with the worn brown carpeting and freshly painted white-beige walls. I waited for Julie to make a move in that direction and, when she didn't, I headed for the couch, letting her follow. Alone with me, she grew quiet, looking uncomfortable. I asked her a series of questions: how her knee was, how old she was, what grade she was in. She gave monosyllabic replies—"okay," "seven," "second"— while casting longing glances at the blackened television set.

Needing an ice breaker, I looked around, then noticed some children's games and a deck of cards on the lower shelf of the coffee table. I asked her what card games she knew, and when she found out I knew Crazy Eights and was willing to play, she began to perk up. She sat on the floor across from the coffee table, her braced leg outstretched, the other leg curled underneath.

She took out the deck of cards, did a few labored shuffles, dealt us each seven, then turned over the top card, a six of diamonds. I didn't have a six, a diamond, or an eight in my hand, so I started drawing cards. I had an incredible run of bad luck and was still unable to put anything down after drawing nine cards.

"You sure you know how to play this game?" asked Julie.

"Yes," I said, drawing another card I couldn't play.

"You're supposed to put down a card like the one . . ."

"I know," I said, drawing again with no luck.

"If you got an eight you can . . ."

"Julie, I *know*," I said, testily, and finally got a diamond which I slapped down on the pile. "*There.*"

Julie's luck was just the opposite of mine, and in a couple of minutes she was out, leaving me with a handful of cards that totaled sixty-five points for her.

"Maybe you haven't played enough," she said.

"I've played enough. Just wait'll the next hand, Big Shot."

She laughed and started piling the cards together. I held out my hand.

"Mom always lets me deal," she said.

"I'm not your mom. Hand them over."

"Geez, you don't have to be a grump," she said, grinning, handing me the cards.

Dealing didn't help me much. I was stuck with thirty-three points this time, making it ninety-eight to nothing. The game was to a hundred.

"What are we playing for?" asked Julie, not quite looking at me.

"What do you mean?" I said, sounding appropriately shocked. "I thought we were playing for fun."

"Mom and I always play for something."

"Like what?"

"I don't know. Sometimes she gives me a quarter if I win." She hesitated, looking as if she knew she might be overdoing it. "Sometimes just a dime."

"What's it cost you when you lose?"

Julie shrugged, as if the possibility were not worth considering. "A penny or something."

"Sounds like you've got a heck of a deal."

"Sometimes I have to do a chore," she admitted, her voice dropping in volume.

"That's more like it." I sat back, considering. "Do you help your mom after a meal? Clearing, dishes?"

"Yeah," said Julie, with a pained look.

"I'll tell you what. We'll play this game to a hundred and fifty. If I win, you have to help your mother after breakfast, and I get to sit down and do nothing. If you win, I'll help your mom, and you can go play."

Julie glanced at the scorecard. "You mean I get to start with ninety-eight points?"

"Yes."

"All right!"

For the next few minutes Julie played with total concentration, the tip of her tongue peeking out periodically from between her closed lips, as if it were another observer giving her assistance. I enjoyed watching her as I went through the mechanical procedure of laying down the cards: she was a cute thing, with the same big beautiful eyes her mother had.

Of course the bet was one I couldn't afford to win, not if I wanted to see Charlie again, and I did; anyway it was designed to get me some time alone with Charlie in the kitchen. I was prepared to throw the game if I had to, but there was no need of that. Julie had that huge lead and, like most kids I'd played cards with, she had incredible luck.

After four more hands she had me, one hundred and fifty-four to forty-eight.

As Julie put down her winning card with a whoop, I noticed Charlie standing in the dining area, watching us.

"Well, look at you two," she said, a look of pleasure and, I thought, amazement on her face.

"Mom, Mom," said Julie, hopping up. "I beat Dave at Crazy Eights, and we had a bet, and he has to do all my work after breakfast, and I get to play."

"Julie, no," said Charlie. "Dave's our guest."

"I always pay off my bets," I said. "And she won fair and square."

"He's not very good at cards," said Julie, then jumped aside with a giggle as I reached out to tickle her.

Brunch was fruit salad, an omelette, bacon, and blueberry waffles, all simply done but delicious. At the table we talked mostly to and about Julie, who, when she'd finished, went racing out the front door as if worried that someone was going to renege on her prize. Charlie offered halfheartedly to do all the cleanup, an offer I refused.

"You sure charmed my daughter," said Charlie, as we started carrying things to the kitchen, "which isn't the easiest thing in the world to do."

"I like her. She's really cute."

I was given the job of scraping the dishes while Charlie put the leftovers in foil or Tupperware containers. Over my shoulder I said: "I'm sorry again about the way last night ended."

"No need to apologize. I understand."

"I'm afraid I must have seemed kind of weird."

Charlie gave a little laugh that blended with the sound of crinkling foil. "If you'd seemed kind of weird, I wouldn't have invited you here. You seemed real upset. I figured maybe you'd just gotten divorced and you still weren't . . ." She paused. "I'm glad you told me."

"Me too. By the way, I don't do that on every date. In case you're willing to give me another chance."

"That an invitation?"

"How about tonight after you finish work?"

"Sure."

"Good."

I started to look over my shoulder at Charlie when I made a bad move with the scraper and slopped some leftover egg onto the thigh of my slacks. I cursed and grabbed for the cloth.

"You having problems over there?" asked Charlie, her words echoing slightly as she leaned into the open refrigerator, putting things away.

"A few," I said, wiping at my pants with the cloth. "But I'll manage."

"You want an apron?"

"Thanks anyway."

Charlie muttered something that sounded like *"men."* I said: "I used to be pretty good at this. I'm a little out of practice."

"Why? You got someone to cook for you?"

"Yeah—Pizza Hut."

The dishes were all scraped. I looked around for a dishwasher and realized I was it. I started filling the sink with hot water and dumped in some liquid soap that smelled like lemon Kool-Aid.

"Who takes care of Julie when you're working?" I asked.

"My mother sometimes. Mostly a high-school girl who lives in the neighborhood. Her home life isn't real pleasant, and she's glad to be here in the evenings. Usually she sleeps on the couch and goes to school from here in the morning. I was really lucky to find her. She's real sweet, and Julie likes her a lot. She doesn't charge me all that much. I feel kind of guilty about that. But as soon as I start my day job I'm going to try to make it up to her, maybe give her some money toward college."

"You said you finish school in December?"

"You remembered that?" said Charlie. "That's nice. Yeah, December. I've already got a job lined up with a small insurance company around here. It'll mean working days, having a little money for once, and getting to spend evenings with

Julie." She shut the refrigerator door and came over to the sink. "You want me to take over the washing?"

"No, I'll do it. You dry. You know where things go." I rinsed a dish and stuck it in the plastic dish rack. "I've been meaning to ask you: What's wrong with Julie's leg?"

There was a slight pause and an almost inaudible sigh. Sadness moved like a shadow across her eyes. "Some of the nerves don't work so good in her right leg. In the knee, but mostly in the foot. She can't move some of the small muscles at all. Other nerves kind of overreact. Spastic they call it. She has a slight foot drop. The brace steadies her leg and keeps the foot up."

"What's that from?"

"When she was two they found out she had a brain tumor."

"Jesus," I said. I swung around toward her. "Is she in any danger now? I mean . . ."

"No," said Charlie, quickly. "That's all taken care of. They operated and got all of it. It wasn't malignant. But it caused some damage, kind of like a stroke. For a while she couldn't move her leg. I mean at all. Gradually she got a lot of control back, but they say what's left is going to be permanent."

"So she'll always have to wear the brace?"

"Maybe not. She can walk without it now, if she takes it slow. But she gets excited and forgets, and then she can fall and hurt herself. Later when she's less of a kid she may be able to go without it."

"That whole thing must have been frightening as hell."

Charlie nodded, swallowing hard. "I was never so scared in all my life. She was so *little*. And we didn't know how it was going to turn out. Every time I think of feeling sorry for Julie, I remind myself of how much worse it could have been." She tried a smile and didn't quite make it. "Of course that doesn't always work."

"She seems like a strong little thing. And happy."

"I think so. I hope so anyway."

We finished up the dishes in silence, then got more coffee

and went into the living room, sitting together on the couch. From where we sat we could see, through the picture window, the Bauer house and part of the church. Mrs. Bauer, wearing a dark housedress, was on the front porch of the house, sweeping.

"I feel so sorry for the Bauers," said Charlie. "I wonder if religion really helps people at a time like this. I hope so."

"You're not religious?"

Charlie shook her head. "No. You?"

"No."

"I guess I tried to be when we found out about Julie. I sure tried to pray. But I couldn't. It just didn't make any sense to me. I mean, it's always seemed to me that the world was too screwed up to have been made by anyone. If there is someone out there who cares what happens to us, wouldn't he have made the world different in the first place? I don't know; maybe that's too simple."

"Not to me it isn't."

The front door of the Bauer house opened, and Bauer came out, moving fast down the steps and out the front gate, saying something to his wife over his shoulder. Bauer went around the side of his house, heading toward the back of the church. Mrs. Bauer went to the end of the porch to follow her husband's progress, calling to him, seeming to get no response. She stared after him for a moment, then started sweeping again, but slowly, as if distracted.

As I watched Bauer disappear behind the church, Charlie asked: "Do you know any better what might have happened to Billy?"

"No. Not really."

"If he was taken by someone, I might have seen the car that was used. Or maybe you know that already."

I turned to her, surprised. "No, I didn't."

"You heard about the orange Volkswagen?"

"Yes. You saw it?"

Charlie nodded. "I was the one who told the police about it. We were sitting in the living room at the time. Julie and me. She was watching something on television. I was doing some sewing. I happened to notice the car out the front window. I can't tell you how many times I've wished I'd taken a better look—seen the person, gotten the license number, something. But I'm not a particularly snoopy person. And there's never been any reason to worry about what goes on in this neighborhood."

"You didn't see anybody at all?"

"No. I just noticed it sitting there. The sun was shining in the window, so I had the drapes shut most of the way. I didn't even see the whole car. I just got a glimpse of it. I don't think I would have noticed it at all if it hadn't been that odd orange color. And I never would have noticed what kind it was if it hadn't been a bug. I'm not much on cars."

"Where was it parked?"

"In front of the Bauers' place. Well, not in front exactly. A little bit down toward the church."

"What time was that?"

"Late afternoon. Maybe four-thirty or five. The police said that was about the time Billy must have disappeared. They showed up in the early evening, going door to door to ask questions. Then they organized a search party. I called Wayne to tell him I wouldn't be working that night, and I went along. At first it was kind of like a party. I don't mean people weren't worried, but we all figured Billy must be around somewhere, and we'd find him before long. But as it got later, that all changed: People got pretty frantic. And, if they were like me, they were also thinking about their own children, what it would be like if they were missing like that. When I finally got home, I crawled into bed with Julie. Just to be close to her. To know she was safe."

Charlie was squeezing her cupped hands together, as if there were something in them she was guarding. I remembered the look of panic she'd had when she'd first seen me with Julie outside her house. I put a hand on her arm and asked: "Did you know Billy well?"

She gave a half nod. "Julie knew him better. She was great with him. Kind of like an older sister. Even when he started getting those scary attacks, she wasn't scared. She was real good for him, I think. The poor little guy didn't have many friends at the end." Charlie cocked her head as if listening to her own words played back. She frowned. "I just realized I'm talking about Billy as if he's dead."

She looked at me as if she wanted me to contradict her. When I didn't, she nodded unhappily and said: "My heart really goes out to his parents. They must feel such despair. I know I would. Billy was such a sweet kid. Gentle, bright, polite. Grateful for anything you did for him. He was the kind of kid you wanted to hug. And protect. But no one could protect him from those awful attacks. Or from this." She gestured vaguely toward the window, as if indicating everything outside it. Then she let the hand fall. "I've never seen a child with such sadness in him. I used to see him staring off sometimes when he didn't know I was looking at him. His expression . . . it was like . . . I don't know . . . like he was seeing the end of the world. It scared me a little. When you see sadness like that you feel that if you get too close to it you might get lost in it. I tried to be nice to him, but a part of me pulled back a little. Not Julie, though. I'm proud of her for that. Though maybe she didn't see him the way I did."

Just as Charlie finished speaking, Bauer reappeared in front of his house. His wife was still on the porch, and he yelled something to her, waving a paper he held in his hand. She stared at him as if she were seeing a ghost, dropping the broom and putting both hands to her chest. Bauer started toward the steps, stopped, turned, and glanced across the street toward Charlie's house. He seemed to hesitate, then started running across the street toward us. I jumped up from the couch and ran to the door, with Charlie following.

"Strickland," said Bauer, breathlessly, as he got to the door. "I saw your car . . . you've got to come . . . something's happened . . ."

"What?"

"Billy's been kidnapped!"

$\triangledown$

Chapter 12

THE BAUERS' DINING ROOM seemed funereal with its polished formality and religious artifacts, with the soft sound of hymns coming from a radio in another room. Across the table, Wernecke and Mrs. Bauer stood grim and still, he in gray, she in black, looking like mourners beside a bier.

"Dear God," whispered Mrs. Bauer.

Next to me Bauer made an impatient sound and stepped forward against the table as if he were planning to walk through it. "Martha, don't you understand? This is good news." He jerked his head toward the ransom note lying open on the table. "This means Billy's all right. Doesn't it, Chief?"

"I hope so," said Wernecke.

Bauer ignored the caution in Wernecke's reply. "Martha, the Lord is answering our prayers. I'm sure of it. He has heard our cries." Bauer gestured heavenward with two open hands. "Praise God: Billy's going to be back with us soon."

But Mrs. Bauer wasn't having any of her husband's optimism. In fact, she looked like she had already seen the worst. Her body slid down onto one of the dining table chairs as if it were falling in slow motion.

"Martha, are you all right?" asked Bauer, anxiously.

Mrs. Bauer didn't respond. She seemed full of rapt attention, yet totally absent, like a mystic having a vision. Whatever it was she saw appeared to trouble her deeply.

"Where'd you find the note, Reverend?" said Wernecke, gesturing with his gray Stetson toward the two typewritten sheets of paper.

For a few moments Bauer just stared at his wife. Then, with obvious reluctance, he turned to Wernecke. "Out in back."

"How'd you know it'd be there?"

"I got a phone call."

"When?"

"About eleven-thirty. The man said they had Billy . . . that I'd better do what they said if I ever wanted to see my son again. He told me to go to the back of the church . . . walk down the trail toward the lake . . . look for three white stones in the path. There'd be an oak tree there with a message up on one of the branches. Then he hung up."

"You have any trouble finding the note?"

"I suppose I fussed over every pebble in the path . . . I was so scared I'd miss the stones. But when I got to them they were obvious . . . and right by a tree. The note was up on a limb of the tree . . . folded, with a rock on top of it. I opened the note and read it and then came running back to the house to tell Martha." Bauer glanced at his wife.

"And call Strickland," said Wernecke, unhappily.

"Chief," protested Bauer, "I saw his car across the street, and after all he has been—"

"Never mind," said Wernecke, waving away the rest of Bauer's explanation. "I suppose I should be grateful that you called me at all."

Bauer's expression turned mildly guilty. "Yeah . . . well, I'm not sure what I would have done if they'd said not to call you. But the note says they expect it. You will do what they say, won't you? You won't try to interfere with—"

"Don't worry," said Wernecke. "We won't do anything to put your boy at further risk."

Wernecke looked down, his eyes skimming over the ransom note. I moved to read over his shoulder.

We got your son. We want $12,500 for him. We got
five auto-teller cards from the Mid-California State
Bank. The card numbers are on the other piece of paper.
Put $2,500 in each acount. Fix it with the bank. I know
we can get $500 a day from each account. Soon as we
get our money you get your boy back. We need ID
numbers for each account. When the bank gives them
to you put them in an ad in the personal section of the
classifieds of the Azalea Sun. Make the ad to B.B. Give
the ID numbers in the same order as the card numbers
on the other page. We know the bank will probably call
the cops. Tell them not to try and pull any tricks. Anyone
tries to fuck us over, you'll never see your boy again.

"All that risk for twelve thousand dollars," said Wernecke,
softly, as if to himself. He turned to Bauer. "Can you get the
money?"

Apparently the question hadn't occurred to Bauer before.
Surprise appeared in his face, just a few steps ahead of panic.
"I don't know . . . we've only got three thousand saved. We
could sell the car . . . but that wouldn't . . . and the church
owns the house." Bauer's head swung from side to side as if
his options were stacked about him in the room. "I don't think
the bank . . . unless the church . . . but they . . ." He started
toward the kitchen. "I'm going to call Warren Hadley."

"Try Frank Edmundson too," I said, to Bauer's back, as
he disappeared through the door.

I turned to ask Wernecke a question, then remembered
Mrs. Bauer, who was still seated at the table. She was staring
at the ransom note, but blankly, as if it had put her into an
hypnotic trance.

"Mrs. Bauer," I said.

"Yes?" Her voice was toneless.

"Are you all right?"

She nodded, but something inside her seemed to protest.
Her shoulders slumped. "I guess . . . I don't feel so well. I
guess I should go lie down."

"Let me help you."

I went around the table to her, putting my hands on the

back of her chair. One of my hands inadvertently touched her shoulder, which contracted away from me, like a snail into its shell. The reaction seemed involuntary rather than rude. I helped pull back the chair as she got to her feet.

"Do you need help getting upstairs?" I asked.

"No," she said, but two unsteady steps convinced her otherwise. "Maybe I do."

I moved up next to her, offering my arm as if to a date at a formal affair. She gave me the briefest of smiles, one that seemed ironic as well as grateful, and she put her hand on my arm. We went to the stairway and began to climb.

"Satan is a great deceiver, Mr. Strickland," she said, out of nowhere, and as casually as if she were dropping a remark about the weather. "He 'deceiveth them that dwell on the earth by the means of those miracles which he has the power to do.' "

"Is that so." I wasn't being sarcastic. She'd caught me off guard, and I didn't know what else to say.

"He tries to make us doubt the voice of the Lord within us. To confuse us. To make what we know seem wrong. But we must not let ourselves be deceived. We 'must walk by faith, not by sight.' "

We reached the top of the stairs and, with a slight pressure of her hand, she guided me to the doorway of a room near the front of the house. It was a large room with a single bed. The lacy curtains, the frilly white bedspread, and the fluffy pink robe hanging on the door gave the room that hyperfeminine look usually found only in the bedrooms of the very young and the very old. It was touching, a side to her I wouldn't have expected. But it was also a little sad, this elderly widow's bedroom for a married woman not much older than I was.

Against the far wall near the bed was a small bookcase filled with Bibles and concordances and Christian paperbacks. Above the headboard of the bed was a picture—almost cartoonlike in its colorful simplicity—of the risen Christ appearing to the disciples. Mrs. Bauer stared at the picture for a time. Her face began to relax, to look almost happy. Then she sensed my watching her. She took her hand off my arm.

"Thank you, Mr. Strickland. I'll be fine now."

I went back down to the dining room and found Wernecke staring at the ransom note.

"Auto-teller cards for a ransom," he said. "Damnedest thing I ever heard."

Wernecke scratched the side of his gray hair. Gray flakes appeared, as if some of the hair had been dislodged. The flakes floated down to his shoulders and disappeared against the flecked gray fabric of his suit.

"I can't decide if the idea is real clever or real stupid," he said. "Clever part is, they can get ransom money out of those auto-teller machines like they're anybody picking up the shopping money. How we gonna spot that? The stupid part is, you just can't get a lot of money out of those machines real fast, not with the withdrawal limits they got. Which is the reason, I guess, that the kidnappers are only asking twelve thousand. But I just can't figure taking all that risk for that little money."

"Isn't using one of those machines like handing your picture over to the police?"

Wernecke blinked at me a couple of times. "You're talking about the cameras hidden in those things." He shook his head. "There're no cameras in the ATMs around here. Area's too low risk. Of course . . . if the guy tried some place like Fresno . . ." Wernecke smiled as he contemplated the thought. Then his smile began to erode. "Trouble is, if they know what they're doing, even that may not help. Judging from the pictures that come over my desk, the cameras in those machines are up above. Guy wears a hat with a brim, or shades his face with a newspaper, you may not get enough for a positive ID. Still . . . anything'd be better than nothing."

"How many branches does Mid-California have?"

Wernecke shrugged. "Don't know. But I bet they have at least fifty. It's a big bank, goes all the way from Sacramento to Bakersfield. Dale Hodgetts can tell us—he's the manager of the Azalea branch. He can tell us about the cameras too."

"So these guys could appear at any one of fifty ATM machines up and down central California, put in their cards, get part of their money, and be gone in a few minutes. If they don't run into cameras, or if they screen themselves well enough, they're not likely to get caught. Not at the machines anyway."

"Yeah. Like I said, that part of it's pretty slick. But the money part's real poor. Seems to me you'd have to be a real idiot to put your dick in a ringer like this for twelve thousand dollars."

"Unless the twelve isn't the end of it. Or unless it's someone out to hurt Bauer or the church. Why kidnap the son of a minister if you're after money? The minister's usually the poorest guy in town."

As if on cue, and as if to protest the description, Bauer came in from the kitchen, calling excitedly that he'd gotten the money. "Warren Hadley is sure the church will agree to cosign a note for five thousand. Frank said he'd cosign for another five. With the three thousand Martha and I have saved, that'll be enough. Praise the Lord!" Bauer ran out of air and took an impatient breath. "Frank's going to call Dale Hodgetts at the bank right away. Warren has to call the other board members. He said he'd meet us at the bank in an hour." Bauer threw out his hands. "I still can't believe it was all so easy. Thanks be to God!"

"Not to mention your friends," I said.

Bauer grinned, knowing he was being needled and not caring. "Yes, indeed. Thank the Lord for my friends."

Bauer went on excitedly for a few more minutes. When he began to calm down, Wernecke asked him to show us where he'd found the note. Bauer went to check on his wife first, returning with the report that she was asleep. Then he took us out the back door.

There was a fairy-tale quality about the small backyard, the way the woods came almost to the fence, as if mystery lay just a step beyond home. The kids in the houses along there must have loved it. But in Billy's case the mystery had stepped out of the woods with a frightening reality.

Just beyond the fence was a small path that had been trampled out of the underbrush over time. The path started behind the houses to our right, then curved away from the Bauer house into the woods.

"I thought you said you started from the church," said Wernecke.

"I did," said Bauer. "It's what they told me to do. But now that I know where it is, this'll be quicker."

We entered the woods. The thick shade looked inviting, but the trees had a kind of hothouse effect, trapping the heat and making the place as steamy as a jungle. Small creatures moved through the underbrush around us, and there were cries of birds overhead. A snake, sunning itself on the path, slithered away as we approached.

We followed the path past the point at which it joined a larger path from the church. Soon Bauer pointed out the tree. At Wernecke's urging we avoided the section of path by the tree, moving into the brush to the right.

"I'll ask the sheriff's department to have a couple of detectives look over the area," said Wernecke, stopping a short distance beyond the tree. "Let's leave it to them."

I glanced down the path in the opposite direction from which we'd come. All I could see were more woods and brush and shade.

"What's down there?" I asked.

"The lake," said Wernecke.

"I want a quick look."

I moved on and heard the others follow. It had been a three- or four-minute walk from Bauer's house to the tree, and in another two to three minutes I got glimpses of water. I came to what looked like a pond, but then saw that it was a secluded inlet of the larger lake. Nailed to a tree by the inlet was a small, unpainted wooden cross. I pointed at the cross, giving Bauer a questioning look.

"We have baptisms here sometimes," he said. "When it's warm en—" Bauer broke off suddenly and gave himself a light slap on the head. "Oh, no."

"What?"

"I forgot all about the service here tomorrow evening."

"You can't mean tomorrow. Tomorrow's Saturday."

"Yes. We do baptisms then so they won't interfere with the regular services."

"You're not going to conduct a service tomorrow, are you? With everything that's happening?"

"Of course not," said Bauer. "I was going to get someone to take my place. I just plain forgot." Bauer's shoulders slumped, as if more weight had been put on them. He reached into the breast pocket of his dark suit and pulled out a notebook and pen. "I'd better write myself a note. My mind just doesn't work these days."

I walked on and in a moment got a look at the whole lake. It was fairly good sized, maybe a half-mile across. The side we were on was relatively undeveloped, but the other side had a beach and some rafts, a boating dock, and some buildings that looked as if they were for concession stands and storage. There were also homes built along the water, many with docks and boats, stretching away on either side of the beach.

I felt a slight breeze off the lake. I lifted my face to it, trying to find a whiff of coolness in that stifling heat. As my eyes closed for a moment, a shrill bird call came from overhead, sounding like a cry of complaint.

Wernecke came up next to me with his own complaints. "Come on, Strickland, this is no time to sunbathe. You ready to go?"

I opened my eyes. "A question first: If the kidnappers took Billy out this way, would they have had to go over there to get to a road?" I pointed to the beach area.

"No. There are roads on all sides of the lake. And all sorts of paths. They could have gotten out in almost any direction."

"Are there houses along those other roads?"

"Some. But there's orchards and farmland too. Easy to get in and out without being spotted. We'll be asking around when it's safe to."

"Seems to me a beach wouldn't be a bad place to steal some ATM cards."

"That and a million other places," said Wernecke impatiently. He shifted his feet, his thick shoulder jostling mine. "Let's go. I want to get back and call Hodgetts. He's going to need some time to set up the payoff. The sooner we get started, the better for Billy."

As we turned to go, there came the cry of that bird again, shrill, insistent, and uncannily human. This time it sounded like the cry of a child in pain.

$\triangledown$

Chapter 13

"**Y**OU MEAN YOU'RE not going to help me get the money?"
Bauer bellowed out the words, looking as if he was about
to burst into tears or strangle someone. Warren Hadley took
a quick step back, glancing around the small bank manager's
office as if it were a trap he had just stumbled into.

"Vernon, I didn't say that. Calm down, will you, please.
If you'd been listening to me, you'd have heard me say that
I *am* authorized to co-sign the note. But I am obliged to tell
you—Vernon, they made it a condition—that several of the
church board members are unhappy at the idea of paying off
these people. They think it's like paying off terrorists. It just
encourages more of the same."

Bauer was staring at Hadley in disbelief. "You mean they
don't want me to pay the kidnappers? They expect me to let
my son *die?*"

Warren Hadley took another step back, stretching his
neck a little as if his shirt collar had just shrunk. He was a
slender, gray-haired man, who would have appeared rather
distinguished except for a certain fussiness that had become
even more pronounced with this confrontation.

"Vernon, no one's *expecting* anything. Of course they
know how you feel about your son . . . how hard this must

101

be for you. But they're asking you to consider the principle here. If you pay these people . . ."

Hadley was stopped by Bauer's expression. It wasn't threatening exactly, but it was unrelenting. Hadley looked around the room for support, found none, and gave a sigh of surrender. He began brushing off his beige summer suit as if he'd just picked himself up off the dirt.

"Well," said Hadley, "I've said what I had to say. Dale, shall we take care of those papers now?"

"Sure," said Dale Hodgetts, who'd been observing the confrontation between his customers with a coolness that surprised me. But then he was an all-around surprise as a bank manager: young, athletic, quick to smile, dressed quite conservatively, but with his clothing slightly askew, like a kid who hadn't been able to resist wrestling at his first dress-up party. I wondered in passing if one of his relatives owned the bank.

Hodgetts got a loan officer and a secretary working on Bauer's loans and then was signaled out of the room by Wernecke. I followed. Wernecke gave me a look that told me he was back to resenting my tagging along, but he didn't try to stop me. The three of us went to a conference room with a huge walnut table and chairs upholstered in a gray cloth that looked as if it could have come from the backs of fore-closed-on executives.

The three of us sat at one end of the table. Wernecke pushed his Stetson out onto the table as if it were his ante for a poker game and looked at Hodgetts. "Any problems with the payoff arrangements?"

"None," said Hodgetts, turning up his empty right hand as if in proof. There was a row of calluses along the top of his palm that probably came from the racquetball racquet I had seen tucked through the loops of an athletic bag in his office closet.

"You've put the five stolen cards in Bauer's name?" asked Wernecke.

"We're doing that now."

"What about the new ID numbers?"

"Should have them for you in about an hour." Hodgetts made a jabbing motion with his left hand, freeing his wrist from the sleeve of his charcoal suit coat. He glanced at his watch. "That should give you plenty of time to get your ad in the paper before the deadline."

"Will the kidnappers be able to use the cards tomorrow?" asked Wernecke.

"Any time after six A.M. At least as soon as they get the ID numbers from your ad."

"Good," said Wernecke, nodding with satisfaction. "By the way, were all the cards reported stolen?"

"Four of them were. We're trying to contact the fifth person now. I'll have my secretary give you all their names, plus copies of the loss reports."

"Where'd they'd say the cards were lost?" I asked.

"They weren't quite sure," said Hodgetts. "One guessed the lake."

"The police will be checking on that," said Wernecke, gruffly, telling me to butt out. He looked back at the bank manager. "I appreciate all the trouble you've gone to, Mr. Hodgetts. I know the Reverend does even more."

"I'm just glad I could help, Chief. I was getting a little worried there for a while—didn't think I was going to get permission. The folks upstairs are pretty nervous about what kind of precedent they might be setting here."

Wernecke snorted. "I don't think they have to worry much about precedents here. There can't be that many people willing to kidnap someone for a few thousand dollars."

Hodgetts shifted uncomfortably in his chair, obviously not sharing Wernecke's joke. "I'm afraid a kidnapper could do a lot better than that, Chief. Obviously your kidnappers assumed that the $500 per day withdrawal limit was built into the ATM system and couldn't be altered—at least without changing the whole system. I can understand that. Up to an hour ago, I thought the same thing. So did all the other management people I talked to. But then I ran into the head technician, and she told me she could raise the limit on any card to any amount we wanted. Simplest thing in the world."

Hodgetts shook his head in bewilderment. "I still can't believe none of us knew that."

"How much do those machines hold?" I asked.

"Between twenty and fifty thousand. Of course, if you were extorting money, you wouldn't dare attract attention by withdrawing a lot at the busy machines. You'd look for deserted ones. Even then you'd have to be careful you didn't look suspicious to a passing patrol car. But if your limit were high enough and you hit the right machines, I'd bet you could get out fifty to a hundred thousand a day per card."

Wernecke gave a low whistle. "Looks like our kidnappers really screwed up."

"You can see now why the idea's got the bank so worried," said Hodgetts, holding his cupped hands in front of him as if they were measuring the worry like flour. "What if someone kidnapped a bank officer and demanded a million dollars via ATMs? What would we do? No one had even thought of that before. We've got no policies, no procedures—I'll bet we're in for a year's worth of meetings on that one." Hodgetts got a glum look, whether at the prospect of kidnappings or meetings.

"So it's safe to say our kidnappers are no high-tech wizards," said Wernecke.

"I suppose," said Hodgetts. "But they could be almost anyone else. As I say, most of the people at the bank didn't know those limits could be raised."

"Speaking of not being high-tech wizards," I said, "I'm just realizing how little I know about ATMs. We were going to ask you about the cameras, but I think we need to know more than that. How about running us through the basics of the system?"

"Sure," said Hodgetts.

"Maybe this would go faster if I tell you first what I already know. I know each machine's like a computer terminal. You put your card in a slot, type in your ID number, get instructions on the screen, and type in your transaction. A record of your transaction comes out one slot. Money, if you're making a withdrawal, comes out another. The idea of the ID number, which you memorize, is to keep anyone else from using your card."

"That's the *idea*," said Hodgetts. "The problem is that a lot of people can't manage to remember their ID numbers, so they write them down on something in their purses or wallets, and then the thief gets the card *and* the number." Hodgetts' disgruntled look shifted to a laugh. "Not that we're always so brilliant ourselves. We made the same sort of mistake at first, mailing out the card and ID number together, so that anyone stealing the envelope from the mail had both. Now we send the card and ID number in separate mailings. Of course the thieves can get around that by checking the same mailbox several days in a row, but it at least makes life a little more complicated for them. You do the best you can." Hodgetts glanced at us as if for sympathy, but immediately his expression turned apologetic. "Sorry. I guess I'm rambling."

"You're doing fine," I said. "You never know what might turn out to be useful."

"How many ATM machines does the bank have?" asked Wernecke.

"Eighty-five. There's one at each of our fifty-seven branches, plus another twenty-eight at places like shopping malls and college campuses."

"What hours?"

"Six in the morning to midnight."

"And that's the same in all locations?"

"Yes. It's one big system. Most things are the same at all locations."

"Not cameras, though," I said.

"No," said Hodgetts. "The bank decided they were only worth the expense in high-risk areas. I'd guess we have about twenty machines with cameras. There are some in Fresno, Bakersfield, Sacramento, Modesto. I think Stockton. I can get you the exact number and locations, if you'd like."

"I'd like," said Wernecke.

"How do the cameras work?" I asked. "I assume if I tried to use a card that was known to be stolen, the machine wouldn't give me any money. And it would—what? Signal the camera to take my picture?"

"First it would eat your card to—."

"Pardon?"

Hodgetts grinned. "Sorry. A little jargon. What I mean is that if a card known to be stolen is inserted, the machine simply pulls the card inside the machine. Takes it out of circulation."

"Clever."

"As for the cameras, those are all VCRs. The machines are activated whenever a transaction takes place, then turned off. They're on for all transactions."

"The still photos you give the police are made from the VCR tape," said Wernecke.

"That's right."

"From the photos that come into the station it looks like all the cameras are positioned overhead."

"In most cases."

"Which makes it relatively easy to block their view—like with a cap pulled way down."

"I guess so," said Hodgetts. "I suppose they couldn't fit the camera in with the other equipment."

"When a stolen card is used, is there an alarm that goes off at a local police station?" I asked.

"No," said Hodgetts. "ATM transactions are over so fast that the odds of catching someone in the act of using a stolen card are almost nil. An alarm system like that wouldn't be effective enough to justify its cost."

"Is there an alarm that goes off inside the bank then?"

"No."

"How does someone know when a stolen card has been used? Someone inside the bank checks the ATM records at the end of the day?"

Hodgetts shook his head. "You got to understand that even though the ATMs are at bank branches—a lot of them anyway—the branches have almost nothing to do with them. At the end of the day the deposit envelopes and the computer tapes and the VCR tape are sent by interoffice mail to a central office where all the transactions are checked. Actually one of two offices, Fresno or Sacramento. If they find something suspicious, security analyzes the situation and sends a report to the police. If there was a camera in operation, security reviews the VCR tapes and gets the appropriate pictures—the computer tapes and the cameras both have clocks in them, and it's a simple matter to correlate them."

"But no one is really monitoring the system while it's in operation?"

"It *is* monitored—twenty-four hours a day. By security people in our central offices." Hodgetts gave me a look that was part frustration, part apology. "I guess I'm not being as clear as I should be. The machines are monitored; they're just not monitored for stolen cards. They're being monitored to make sure they're in operation. There are alarms that go off in the central office but only related to operational problems. Like vandalism."

"In other words, if I took a baseball bat to one of the ATMs, that would set off an alarm. But not if I tried to use a stolen card."

"Exactly. If the machine's down, the customers who try to use it get annoyed, and we risk losing their business. We've got to get someone out there to fix it. There's not the same urgency with a stolen card. If we know it's stolen, the machine's eaten the card, and the person's gone. Rushing isn't going to do much good. Or so the bank feels."

"So there won't be any way for us to find out about the activity on these cards until the end of the day when the tapes are reviewed?" asked Wernecke.

"Actually, they're not reviewed until the next day, maybe the day after."

"Great," said Wernecke, with a groan.

Hodgetts shrugged. "Hey, Chief, we're in the business of banking, not law enforcement."

"Yeah, I know," said Wernecke, giving Hodgetts a conciliatory look. "What do you think, though? Could the bank fix up the computer to signal your security office when one of the stolen cards is used so they can let me know?"

"I'm sure it's possible. Whether they'll do it will depend on how involved it is."

"Ask 'em, will you," said Wernecke, getting to his feet and grabbing his Stetson from the table. "I'd like to know as quickly as possible whether the kidnappers are picking up their money. And where. Though, frankly, unless those guys run into a camera, I don't think we're going to get much help from your security system."

$\triangledown$

Chapter 14

I STEPPED OUT OF the newspaper office into the fierce afternoon sunlight. Bits of glare off metal and glass struck my eyes like fragments of an explosion. I pressed my eyelids shut. Red afterimages spread through my mind like wounds.

I stepped back into the shade of the overhang, bumping into Bauer who had followed me out. I mumbled an apology and moved to the side, waiting for my sight to clear.

When I could see again, I looked at Bauer, thinking he'd be impatient to be going. Instead he was standing stiff and still, staring into the distance with eyes unfocused, like a statue of a saint in contemplation.

"We've done all we can do," he whispered to someone out there. God, maybe. Or the kidnappers. Or Billy.

Whoever it was wasn't answering, because after a moment Bauer frowned and turned to me. "Strickland," he said, his voice full of ache, "am I ever going to see my son again?"

The question caught me off guard. It was Bauer who had been all optimism a few hours before. He was the man of faith. What the hell was he asking me for?

I started to give him some phony encouragement, but something severe in his expression told me that wasn't what he wanted. Finally I said: "Look, I don't know. It depends on too many things: who these people are, what they really want, whether they've managed to handle their side correctly, whether the ransom pickup goes all right. Not knowing any of that, I'd have to say the odds are about fifty-fifty."

"Odds," said Bauer, with a halfhearted attempt at sarcasm. "You make life sound like a crap game."

I shrugged. "You've got my odds. Maybe God can give you better ones."

"I hope so." Bauer didn't sound as sure of that as I would have expected. "Thanks for being honest."

"No need to thank me," I said. "The fact is, I feel like apologizing."

"No need for that either." Bauer shifted his feet and coughed to clear his throat. "By the way, I'm glad you're in on this thing."

I looked at him in surprise. "Why? All I've managed to do so far is annoy people."

Bauer smiled. "You've done that, all right. But you've been open with me. I feel I can be open with you. There aren't many people around here I could say that about."

"I'm safe because I'm a stranger."

"Yes. But there's more than that. You also remind me some of myself when I was younger."

"Before you got religion."

"Before I found the Lord."

I'd known before he'd spoken that he'd correct that phrase I'd used. Shades of some old family game.

"There's something else," said Bauer. "Something you won't like hearing. Since Billy's been missing, I've had moments of feeling abandoned by God. A lot of Christians have had moments like that. Even our Lord did, in the garden. I guess I do what everyone does in that situation—look for signs of God's hand. Your coming here—you with your bitterness against God—helps me feel that the Lord really is working out His purposes in this."

I pressed my eyes shut again, this time in exasperation. "Reverend, if you're looking for your God to do miracles with Billy, I'll be rooting for you all the way. But if you're looking for Him to do miracles with this boy, you'd better just forget it."

Bauer laughed, a little embarrassed, but still sure of himself. "Isn't there a line in Shakespeare about protesting too much?"

"Yeah. But there ought to be a line about preaching too much. Let's go."

I started walking, and Bauer came with me, both of us heading toward the bank, where my car was parked. Bauer had been driven to the bank earlier, and I was the only one left to drive him home. Wernecke hadn't gone with us to place the ad, afraid his presence might alert the paper that something newsworthy was happening.

The downtown sidewalk was broad, but the shade from the heavy wooden awnings was not, and we tried to keep close to the stone buildings, out of the worst of the heat. People coming from the other direction had the same idea, and there were lots of dodgings and apologies as we made our way up the street. It was only because of these maneuvers that I noticed the woman.

She was a short blonde, probably in her early thirties, though it was hard to tell her age. Her figure beneath the scoop-necked yellow blouse and white skirt was on the borderline between slender and wasted. Her face was close to being pretty but was marred by the kind of lines you see on the faces of people who've lost a lot of weight.

There was nothing exceptional about her looks, or about the looks of her companion—a heavyset, heavy-bearded man, wearing a clean blue work shirt and freshly washed jeans with traces of old grease stains. What was exceptional was the look the woman gave Bauer. It was pure venom.

Bauer stumbled slightly as he saw the woman and muttered something that sounded like "Mart." Her face blazed in response, then she tugged at the hand of her companion, and they were gone.

I waited for half a minute for Bauer to speak. When he didn't, I asked him who the woman had been. He just kept walking. I asked him again, with a lot less gentleness, and he shook his head.

"Cut the crap," I said, stopping. "You tell me who that

woman is or I'm going back there and catch her and find out
for myself."

"No!" said Bauer, half-frantic, grabbing at my forearm.

"You'll tell me?"

"Yes."

I looked around for a place where we could talk, out of the
heat, and saw a coffee shop across the street. I grabbed
Bauer's arm in turn. "Come on."

The coffee shop was dim and cold, and mostly empty. We
went to a back booth with a Formica-topped table covered
with change and crumbs. A waitress cruised by, giving us a
smile. She took the change and left the crumbs.

"What's the woman's name?" I asked.

Bauer hesitated a moment, then spoke the name as if it
hurt him to say it. "Marj Hempell."

"Tell me about her."

"She wouldn't do anything to Billy. She loves children."

"Just tell me. If she's done nothing, she's got nothing to
worry about."

The waitress came back, this time with a cloth, and wiped
the table. She started to chat about the weather, then saw
that neither of us was in the mood. She took our drink orders
and left.

"Tell me about her. What happened? And when?"

Bauer's eyes searched the room, as if he were looking for
a last way out. Then he gave a sigh and settled back against
the booth cushions.

"It happened three years ago," he said. "Marj was a member of our church. She taught Sunday school. She was real
different then: friendly, energetic, pretty. Popular with everyone, especially the children."

Bauer paused as the waitress appeared again. She put an
iced tea in front of him and a Coke in front of me and went
away without conversation. Bauer looked in the direction of
his glass and grimaced, as if it were full of some bitter medicine he was being asked to drink. After a moment he said:
"Marj was married then, to a man named Larry. An auto
mechanic. He came to church with Marj, but he wasn't a

real committed Christian. He drank some, liked to have a good time with the boys. Still, as far as anyone could tell, he was a pretty good husband and father. They had three children—two boys and a girl.

"One day Marj came to me and told me she was planning to divorce Larry. She said they hadn't been close for years, couldn't communicate, that sort of thing. She wasn't coming to me for counseling. She just wanted me to know before she filed. Before it became public knowledge. I was against the divorce, as she knew I would be. Our church is against divorce for Christians."

"Why just for Christians?"

"The Bible tells us that marriage is a sacred covenant to be entered into for all eternity. A Christian would knowingly enter into such a covenant before God. A non-Christian would not. It's a matter of intent. We would never encourage anyone to get divorced. But divorce could be condoned for a non-Christian. Not for a Christian."

"You don't condone divorce for a Christian under any circumstances?"

"No. Separation, but not divorce."

"Much like the Catholics."

Bauer gave me a slight smile. "I suppose so. We can't be different in everything."

"Go on."

"Marj said she knew she'd have to resign her position with the Sunday school, but she wanted to keep coming to church, if things didn't get too unpleasant. She asked me if I'd forbid her coming. I told her that as long as I was pastor, no one would be forbidden to come to my church."

"Would some churches actually do that?"

"It's a common practice among some fundamentalist congregations. It's always seemed to me cruel and stupid. Why cut someone who's in error off from one of the sources of God's light?" Bauer glanced beyond me toward the front windows, squinting a little at the glare. "Not that she was seeing that light. I explained to her why divorce was wrong, but she wouldn't accept that. She said she was very unhappy and didn't believe a God of love would want her to be un-happy. I told her it wasn't that simple, but to her it was.

"I suggested couples counseling, but she said they'd done that already. I asked her to pray about it, and she said she'd done that too. I kept badgering her—I was concerned for her and I think she could see that—and finally I got her to agree to see me for five counseling sessions before she made her decision.

"At the first session she told me about an affair she'd had one time during her marriage. I think she told me as a way of trying to let me know how unhappy she'd been. She said she hadn't enjoyed it much—she'd been feeling too guilty, too afraid of getting caught—but there were some things she'd had with that man that made her see more clearly what she'd been missing with her husband. Not the physical things. A certain intimacy.

"I didn't dwell on the affair, didn't condemn her for it. It was wrong, but she knew that . . . and it was over . . ."

For a moment Bauer's voice faded out, and his mind wandered off. Whatever it was he was thinking about seemed to add some pain to his eyes.

". . . It was over, and the past wasn't the point. The point was what she was going to do now.

"After the second counseling session, Marj had to go to Oregon to be with her sick mother. She was gone over three weeks. By the time she got back, I was preparing to leave for a month myself. I'd signed up for a short counseling course at a Bible college in Grand Rapids, Michigan, and Martha and I were going to combine that with a visit to family in Ohio. I'd hoped that the crisis with her mother might make Marj rethink her plan to divorce, but it had only strength-ened her resolve. I had the feeling that she wanted to get those last three counseling sessions out of the way as fast as possible—to fulfill her promise to me—so she could get on with the divorce.

"I'd arranged for a young divinity student to fill in for me while I was gone. His name was Ned. He'd just graduated from theological school in southern California and was due to become pastor of a small church in Montana. I had interviewed him at some length, and he'd seemed to me an intelligent, sensitive, upstanding Christian.

"When I refused to let Marj out of her commitment to those three remaining counseling sessions, she asked me if I'd allow her to have them with the substitute pastor. I hadn't had any success with Marj, and I thought maybe the new man could get through to her in a way I could not.

"Ned arrived a couple of days before I was due to leave, so I could fill him in on his duties. I told him about Marj and a couple of other people I was counseling. That's standard practice when one counselor fills in for another. We discussed the cases at some length, and, believe me, he didn't say anything that could have told me what might happen."

Bauer's face took on a look of appeal, but immediately he shook his head, as if denying his own petition. His eyes shut briefly in a kind of hopeless look.

"That first counseling session with Ned must have been a nightmare for Marj. Before she could say anything, he told her that he knew about her affair. He called her a whore, cursed by God." Bauer winced and tapped his closed fist against the edge of the table. "The idiot. He said that he was going to tell her husband and that he was going to denounce her from the pulpit the next Sunday."

"Why was he going to denounce her from the pulpit?" I asked.

"It's done in some churches. Not many, but some. Given what I knew of Ned's background, given what he'd said to me, I never guessed that he . . . But I should have found out. It was my business to find out."

Bauer bit down on his lip, not idly, but hard, as if administering some small punishment.

"What happened then?" I asked.

"Marj was beside herself, of course. She began pouring out her heart to some people she trusted. One was an aunt who lived out of state, whose husband was an attorney. The husband called Ned and told him that if he spoke against Marj from the pulpit he would be violating a professional confidence—that he and the church would be in serious legal trouble. Fortunately Ned had sense enough to listen. There was no public denunciation."

"Where was the harm then?"

"Ned had already told the husband. And what Ned didn't dare do in public, he did in private. He convinced Larry that his wife was wicked and would corrupt the children. Only the Lord can judge Larry, but the man's transformation was suspiciously convenient. Suddenly he became the model Christian. He stopped drinking. Stopped going out with the boys. Started participating in all the church activities. He hadn't been all that involved with the kids from what I understand, but suddenly he was the model father. He bought the children new clothes and started taking them everywhere. He was always playing the martyr, crying on people's shoulders and pulling them over to his side. And poisoning the children against their mother.

"There was a custody hearing, and Larry paraded in a bunch of church members to testify against his wife. A lot of them were her old friends and that made their testimony that much more believable to the judge. I don't know that there were lies, though I've heard there were. I hope not. But it wouldn't have taken lies. Those hearings are so subjective. Those people felt she was wicked and unfit, and that's what they said. Marj apparently didn't understand what was happening until it was too late to make much of a defense. She lost the kids, and I think it almost killed her."

Deep pain showed in Bauer's eyes. He shook his head and kept on shaking it for a few moments, as if he were trying to deny the event out of existence.

"I didn't find out what had happened between Ned and Marj until I'd been back from vacation for a few days and called her. She screamed at me over the phone, blaming me for what had happened. When I tried to explain my side, she hung up on me. She was right too. Whatever my excuses, Ned was my responsibility.

"Later on, maybe I should have known about the plotting that was going on right under my nose with Larry and some of the congregation. But I didn't know. I'd like to think that perhaps they were keeping it from me because they knew I wouldn't go along. I couldn't believe it when I heard about what had happened in the custody hearing. I knew Marj must be feeling desperate, so I went over to her house, hoping there was something I could do to help. I got to see her for about fifteen seconds before she slammed the door in my face."

Bauer grimaced and looked down. He rubbed a hand across his forehead, then down over his eyes. "I don't think I'll ever forget the way she looked at me. I've committed a lot of sins in my life, made a lot of mistakes, hurt a lot of people. But never have I felt such hatred from another human being. Never."

$\triangledown$

Chapter 15

THE BAR WITH ITS shadows and noise had an aura of dreams, but not of good dreams. I was tired, and I shouldn't have been drinking tired. But it was the songs, finally, that brought it on, sad songs that got me thinking of Katie.

By the time the songs were over, the depression was there, rawness pressing against my insides like an incipient explosion. Closing my eyes, I tried to obliterate the feeling by silencing all thought, like an inept repairman trying to disconnect a circuit by ripping out every wire he could find. I couldn't disconnect it completely, but gradually the pain began to diminish.

"Hey, Dave."

The words came with the light poke of a finger to my ribs, and I opened my eyes to see Charlie just in front of me, all red hair and freckles. I felt myself smile in spite of myself.

"Sorry I haven't been over much," she said. "This place has been such a zoo."

"I know. It's okay. We'll make up for it later."

"For sure." Someone at one of the tables hollered her name, and she gave me a helpless smile. "Gotta go."

Turning, Charlie bumped into a woman who was returning from the restroom to the barstool next to me. There were apologies, then hellos, then, as an afterthought, a rushed introduction.

"Sharon, this is my friend, Dave," said Charlie. "Dave, Sharon—Jim's sister."

I waved as Charlie moved off, then turned to Sharon, a skinny young woman with dark hair cut short and boyish. She was wearing a bright new western shirt like the usual make-believe cowpokes, but her jeans and boots had seen some real work.

It had taken a moment for me to absorb the introduction. "You're the singer's sister?"

"Un-huh."

"What about you? What do you do?"

Sharon stretched her lower leg out from the barstool and stared at her boot, almost as if she were verifying her identity. "I got a ranch," she said, in a voice that was barely above a mumble. "I board horses. Do some training. Give lessons."

"Sounds nice."

"Un-huh."

I noticed that she wasn't wearing a wedding ring. "Nice that you've got your own business at your age."

She glanced down at her left-hand ring finger and began massaging it as if it were bruised. "It was my husband's and mine," she said. "Before we got divorced."

She lapsed into a gloomy silence. I glanced up at the bandstand, my eyes falling on the stocky kid with the long blond hair and cowboy hat who was playing bass.

"Too bad about what happened to the other bass player," I said. "How's he doing?"

"Not too good," said Sharon. "His leg's broke real bad."

"Anyone figure out why those guys hurt him?"

The quick, hard shake of her head seemed more a rejection of the question than an answer to it. One of her boots twitched down toward the floor as if she was about to make an exit.

"Your brother's quite a songwriter," I said, making one last try. "Where'd he learn to write like that?"

The boot lifted. Sharon turned to me with a smile, and her whole face seemed to open up. Obviously I'd hit on what was for her a very special topic.

"Jim's always been good with words," she said, her voice clear and chatty now. "Maybe got it from my mom. She used to write poetry when she was younger. Before she got religion." Sharon gave her eyes a slight roll. "Jim went to JC for a year. Took a bunch of English classes. That helped him some."

"Charlie tells me he'd like to take some stuff to Nashville."

"He wants to. He's been sending some tapes of his stuff. But you can't do nothin' long distance like that. You got to be there. That's what the Nashville people say. I sure hope he can get there someday."

The band started playing their break song to announce the end of the last set. Hadley did his usual patter about folks drinkin' up and comin' back soon, and then the stage was silent. Hadley took off his guitar and leaned it against the amp. As he did so, he noticed his sister waving at him.

"Hey, Shar," he said, waving back. "We're going to a party tonight. Want to come?"

"Sure!"

"Give me a hand packing up?"

"Okay."

Sharon hopped off the stool and rushed over to the bandstand, as enthusiastic as a seven-year-old whose big brother has just asked her to play.

I sat sipping draft beer and listening to the jukebox until Wayne kicked us all out, then went to my car to wait. I entertained myself by watching the crowd file out back—the happy drunks, the quarrelers, the couples tangled together as if they were already in bed, and one poor sap who kept pushing a proposition up to the point where the girl's car kicked gravel in his face.

Gradually the parking lot cleared out, leaving dust clouds swirling in the sickly yellow light. I began to feel the depression poking its way back into my gut. It was a relief to see Charlie come out the door.

She rushed across the lot and got in the passenger door with a slightly out-of-breath "hi." I leaned over to give her a quick kiss and she leaned toward me to help, but we turned our heads the wrong way and caught noses like two children trying to figure out how kissing works. We laughed and tried it again, this time making a mock-serious show of getting the noses and lips just right. But if it started mock, it ended serious. When we finally pulled apart, her face looked as flushed as I felt.

"So . . ." said Charlie, drawing out the word as if it were an entire sentence, as she sat back, looking at me, patting at her hair. "You gonna jump my bones or what?"

A sharp laugh came out of me. And nothing else.

"I embarrass you?" she asked, after a moment.

"Surprised me, anyway."

"I guess women of your generation aren't so blunt."

"My generation, huh."

"Now don't get touchy. So you're a little bit older than I am."

"That doesn't bother you?"

Charlie shook her head. "My dad was fifteen years older than my Mom. Chad was seven years older than me. I've always gone out with older guys." She looked at me, then got a mischievous look. "So . . . now that that's out of the way . . . ?"

I wanted to say yes, had wanted to ask her before she'd asked me, but something held me back. After a moment I saw her bravado begin to wilt in the silence.

"Hey," she said, with a shrug, shifting around in her seat. "If you don't feel like it, that's okay. Maybe I shouldn't have just come out with it like that. I guess a lot of guys don't like that. But I want you to know I don't just go around doing that. I happen to like you a lot."

Her vulnerability got to me in a way her bravado hadn't, and I put aside the hesitancy I was still feeling. I reached out and cupped her chin with my hand and turned her face back.

"Charlie, I like you too. A lot. And I've wanted to put my hands on you since the first moment I saw you—even with that ridiculous curler hanging off the back of your head."

Charlie laughed, reaching up to her hair as if she were worried that the curler was still there. "It's just that I . . ." I stopped myself. "Let's. I'd like to."

"You sure? You know it would be okay if . . ."

I put a finger to her lips to stop the protest. Then I drew myself up in a parody of a southern gentleman. "Miss Charlene, may I have the honor of jumping your bones?"

We made a bunch of dumb jokes as we drove across the street and went into my motel room, the jokes making it all more comfortable. I was feeling good as I hopped into bed, while Charlie went into the bathroom. But as I lay by myself under the covers in the silence, it all started to go wrong. The dim light in the room seemed to get suddenly dimmer, and the rawness came back into my stomach and chest.

Charlie started joking again as she got into bed, but I stopped that by holding her close and kissing her slowly. I wanted to get on with this, not out of any sexual urgency now, but out of the fear that the oncoming depression would spoil it.

When the kiss stopped, she pulled her head back a little, putting her hands on both sides of my face, adjusting the distance between us as if I was something that wouldn't quite come into focus. I noticed that her eyes were moist.

"That was nice," she said. "I guess maybe you do like me."

"I like you a lot, Charlie. Come here."

I had a sudden longing to be close to her, but the urge seemed to stifle itself, in the same way that panic sometimes stifles the ability to run. I could feel the steel casing forming around my heart, and inside was the sadness, weighing me down, making it all an effort. I tried to fight it off, but I couldn't. My body began to feel heavy and the touches I received felt almost painful. My insides were all raw. I pulled back from Charlie slowly, patting her arm as I did so, trying to give her some sort of reassurance.

"It's no good. I can't."

"What's the matter?" she asked, looking startled, shifting up on one elbow. "Is it something I did?"

"No. It's not you. It's me."

"You sick?"

"No. Not the way you mean. I just feel . . . shitty inside."

"This have to do with your wife?"

"I wasn't thinking about her just now. But it must."

"It's been two years," she said, with exasperation. Then she winced. "Sorry. That was cold. I'm sure you loved her a lot."

"I did. But it's not that. It's the way it ended."

We sat up against the headrest, and I put my arm around her. We sat there for a time, and it should have felt nice, but it didn't; the room just felt cold and bleak. Charlie made some stabs at getting me to talk, but I couldn't. I kept feeling that if I opened up, pieces of myself would come exploding out of my mouth. Eventually we both gave it up, saying reassuring things that we knew neither of us believed as we got ourselves dressed. I drove her home and walked her to the door, and it was a relief to see the baby-sitter asleep on the couch because that meant I didn't have to make a pretense of coming in and making more of this dismal conversation. I gave her a peck on the cheek and apologized again and then left abruptly, almost angrily, not bothering to look back or wave.

I expected to feel relief as I drove away, but what I felt instead was a loss so sharp I was sure for a moment I was going to vomit. I yanked the car to the curb next to an empty field. I pushed at the car door to get out, but it was too late, only what came out was an explosion of tears. "Damn you," I said over and over, looking out into the empty night, not even knowing for a moment whom I was talking to, but continuing to talk aloud.

"Damn it, Katie, didn't you ever think about how it was going to be for me? You had to know I'd be the one to find you. How could you do that to someone you loved? You had no right. Do you know how long it took me to get that moment out of my mind? I used to look at pictures of you for hours, trying to blot it out, like I was throwing things on something I wanted to bury. But it never worked. I'd close my eyes and there you'd be in that bath. God, Katie, there was so much blood.

"Did you ever think how it would be for me later? Walking around like I was the last person on earth because the only two people I cared about were gone. Nothing to do but keep going over it—wondering what I could have done that would have made a difference. And missing you so bad. I'd never felt pain like that before. I used to sit in my chair at night with my gun next to me, and I'd think: This is the last night I'm going to go through this. But I never pulled the trigger. I'm not sure why. Maybe I was too pissed off at you. I'd think to myself: This is what she was really doing, killing us both. And then I'd get mad.

"Why didn't you give me a chance? Why didn't you let me try to help? You wouldn't let yourself be held, you wouldn't talk to me. You just . . . went off. Didn't you ever think, hey, this guy's hurting too? And even if he doesn't feel just the same about the baby as I do, he loves me and he's worried sick about me and it wouldn't hurt to try just a little.

"Did you ever think about me at all? Jesus, Katie, how could you have loved me and done what you did? Sometimes I get so pissed off I wish you were here just so I could wring your goddam neck."

There was a fresh burst of tears. When they began to subside, I brushed at my eyes and looked off into the night. After a time I got an image of Katie sitting across a room from me—our living room probably. The room itself was vague, though Katie's image was clear. She was looking at me as if she were listening, those intelligent gray-blue eyes of hers focused on me, her head tilted, her forehead knitted ever so slightly. Then, as if something inside had distracted her or called her away, her eyes turned inward to some other place, and she was there and yet gone. I felt that old familiar pang.

"Katie, I sometimes wonder if we were ever really together. There were so many places in you I couldn't go. I still don't know what was there. Probably sad places—selfish, the way sad places are. You'd think it would make it easier, saying good-bye, that we were maybe never quite together. But it's made it harder to let you go, because it feels like a defeat, like I've been cheated out of something. I want you back so we can finish what we started. But it's never going to be. And I've got to make myself see that.

"I've got to say good-bye, Katie. I know it's not going to be this easy, that I'll probably have to say the good-byes lots of times to make them stick, but I'm making a start. I love you. I'm sorry for your pain. I'm sorry if there was something I didn't do that I should have done. But I've got to get on."

I brushed my sport-coat sleeve across my eyes and started the car and turned it around. When I got up to Charlie's front door it was all dark inside except for a light in the kitchen, and I thought I'd have to make more noise than I wanted, but then I saw her through the crack in the almost closed kitchen door, sitting at the table, staring off at the wall. I tapped softly, trying not to wake the baby-sitter, but I wasn't quiet enough and the girl stirred on the couch. Charlie came rushing out of the kitchen, telling the baby-sitter it was all right, to go back to sleep. At the front door she flicked on the porch light till she got a glimpse of me blinking against the light with eyes that must have looked like hell, and then she turned off the light and stepped outside.

"I'm an idiot," I said, with a voice that wasn't quite making it. "But not enough of an idiot to want to walk away from you."

"I knew there was something about you I liked," she said, and she took my hand and pulled me inside.

$\triangledown$

Chapter 16

T HE GLARE OF THE sun accentuated the dilapidation of the small farm. The white paint on the one-story house was peeling, and pieces of the shake roof dotted the ground like so many fallen leaves. The corral fence looked like it would topple with a good nudge, but the speckled mare inside didn't look as if she had a good nudge left in her. The yard around the house was all dirt, ruts and gravel, and there were enough disabled vehicles to make the place look like an auxiliary junkyard. The only beautiful thing in sight was a large German shepherd, and it looked nasty.

I'd been watching the Hempell place for most of the day. It was a long shot, but I only had two suspects and I knew the police would be watching Tuttle. From my surveillance I knew that Hempell and her male friend had been home all day, and from a pay-phone call to Wernecke I knew that someone had started using the stolen auto-teller cards. So if Hempell and her friend were in on the kidnapping, they were doing neither the holding nor the pickup. Still, there didn't seem to be any harm in going in for a closer look at them. Any pretext would do as long as it made no mention of kidnapping, which wasn't yet public knowledge.

I pulled into the driveway and parked next to an old Mustang set on blocks. Just in front of it was an old brown Dodge pickup, under which someone was working. I got a glimpse of a bare male belly, the top band of blue Jockey shorts, some grease-stained jeans, and work boots. As I got out of the car, the chained dog upped the volume of its barking. The man under the pickup cursed, then wriggled out from beneath it. He stood up, shifting his two wrenches to one hand, and looked me over. He was a large, black-bearded man in his early thirties, the man I'd seen with Marj Hempell the day before.

"I'm looking for Mrs. Hempell," I said. "This the right house?"

"What'd you want with her?"

"You her husband?"

"No. But I live here."

"I have some business I'd like to discuss with her."

"What business?"

"I think I should speak to her directly."

"Sure. Go right ahead."

As he spoke he glanced toward the house and grinned. I now saw that the leash of the German shepherd was attached to a long wire that came close enough to the front door so that I'd have to get by it to get there.

I gave him my concession in the form of a short laugh. "I guess you've got me there. I don't suppose you'd like to call off the dog."

"You're right," he said, enjoying himself in a sullen sort of way. "I wouldn't."

"Is there any way I get to talk to Mrs. Hempell?"

"I don't know. You might try showin' some manners and tellin' me what you want."

I was trying to decide what I wanted to tell him when I was saved the trouble. A plaintive woman's voice from inside the house yelled, "What's going on out there?" Without waiting for a response, she came rushing out onto the porch, jumping a little as the screen door slammed behind her. She yelled, "Sparky, shut up," at the dog, which immediately gave up its barking for a low growl. Then the woman turned toward us.

"I just now dozed off," she complained, talking about a nap obviously, since it was two in the afternoon and she was wearing a blue sundress. "You know how much I need my sleep. How can I get any sleep around here with all this noise?"

There wasn't much to say to that and neither of us tried. After a moment she asked: "What's going on?"

"Guy here says he wants to talk to you," said the man.

The woman got a nervous look. Her eyes went to the dog, then to the man, reassuring herself that she had allies. She started across the yard, her eyes on my face.

I remembered the words that Bauer had used to describe Marj Hempell before her troubles: friendly, energetic, pretty. What might once have been friendly energy had turned jittery, frantic, fearful, as if she had taken too many amphetamines. The jitters had spoiled her classically featured face, over-thinning it, sketching dark lines under the eyes and worry lines in the forehead, giving a pinched look to her mouth.

"What is it?" she said, stopping about ten feet away from me. "What do you want?"

"You're Mrs. Hempell?"

"Yes. Who are you?"

"My name's Dave Strickland. I'm a private investigator hired to look into the Bauer boy's disappearance."

Mrs. Hempell's shoulder gave an involuntary jerk, and she looked quickly at the man. I heard the man shift his feet and curse under his breath. I kept my eyes on her.

"What do you want with me?" she asked.

"You folks know, of course, that the Bauer boy has been missing for some days. I'm going around talking to some of the church members, past and present, trying to get some idea what might have happened. I'm wondering, for instance, if you know of anyone who might have had it in for Bauer or his son?"

There was silence for a moment as the two of them stared at each other. The woman's eyes seemed to be pleading for something. The man gave a low, disgusted laugh.

"Mister, you're a damned liar."

"How so?" I asked, in a tone of surprise, not offense.

"You know how so," he said. "I think you know damn well what Bauer did to Marj, and what you really want to know is whether she did something to his kid. Isn't that right?"

He was right, of course, but agreeing with him would have sounded too close to an accusation. He looked like he wanted to be provoked, and provoking him would only get me a quick trip out of there.

"No," I said.

"What do you mean, no," said the man, annoyed. "You mean to tell me you don't know what that bastard Bauer did to Marj?"

"I did hear something about some troubles she had with the church," I said. "But I'm not real clear about what they were. Anyway, I thought the trouble had to do with some other minister."

I didn't expect either of them to quite believe me. But Marj Hempell was a victim, and I was hoping that her compulsion to talk about what had been done to her would override any skepticism she might have.

Her fingers fidgeted for a time with one of the folds of her dress. Then she seemed to reach a decision. She turned to the man, whom she called "Bert," and asked for a cigarette. He pulled a rumpled pack of Camel filters out of the pocket of his jeans, gave her one, and lit it for her with a disposable lighter. She took two quick drags and turned toward me. A change seemed to come over her face. The nervousness was still there, but it seemed to come forward now, rather than retreating.

"Those people at the church stole my children away from me," she said.

Bert cleared his throat with a cough. "Hon, you don't have to talk to his guy."

She waved him off with the hand that held the cigarette, causing a small shower of ashes. "They had no cause to do that. I loved those kids so much. I was a good mother. A really good mother. So what if I wanted a divorce? A person's entitled to a little happiness. That didn't mean I wasn't a good mother."

"Hon . . ."

"I knew they wouldn't like it, but I never thought they'd do what they did. They're supposed to be Christians, aren't they? Christians are supposed to be kind, aren't they?"

"What did they do?" I asked.

"I *told* you," she said, with a frantic, teary impatience. "I just told you."

"Yes, but how? How'd they steal your kids away?"

Marj took another drag from her cigarette, blew a puff of smoke to the side, then dropped the cigarette in the dirt, letting it smolder there.

"They got me to trust them and tell them things, and then they told my husband, and they got everybody against me. I didn't know about it till it was too late. I figured I'd get the kids. The mother should get 'em, right?" As she spoke her voice sped up, rising in pitch, until she had to stop to catch her breath. "Everybody knows that children belong with their mother. I figured I had nothing to worry about. I didn't even know Larry *wanted* them. He sure never paid much attention to them when we were together—he was always off somewhere with those buddies of his drinking and playing cards. He was never much of a father. Who was gonna give them to *him?* But then all those people started coming into court telling the judge how terrible I was, and how good Larry was, telling the judge things they weren't supposed to know. I hadn't done anything real bad, but they made it all sound terrible. And they made things up—they *lied*, lied in court, all those people who were supposed to be Christians. I didn't know they were all gonna be there talkin' about me—I didn't have any time to get any answers ready—" She put a hand to her chest, panting as if she'd just finished running. "But anyway I figured it was all so ridiculous, the judge was never gonna believe 'em. But he did, damn him, he did. He took my babies away from me."

Marj dabbed at her moist eyes, smearing mascara over one

lower lid and cheekbone. Bert moved over to her, laying a hand on her shoulder.

"Easy there," he said. "You know you ain't supposed to get all worked up."

"Did you appeal?" I asked, wanting to get more questions in before the flow of talk got cut off.

Marj tried to make a sarcastic sound, but it came out more like a sob. She pushed away from Bert, not rudely, but like someone who couldn't bear to stand still, who couldn't talk without the free use of her arms.

"Oh, I appealed, all right."

"Cost her a fortune," said Bert.

"I thought for sure some other judge would see the wrong that was done to me and make it right," said Marj. "But nothing changed."

"Those judges are all buddy-buddy," said Bert. "They all belong to the same country club. No way one of them's gonna tell another one he's wrong."

"My lawyer told me the law in custody cases isn't real clear," said Marj. "He said it's so subjective, it's hard to get a decision changed. I told him I didn't care, I wanted to try. I kept after them, all of them—the judges, the mediators, the evaluators. They all had the same attitude: didn't want to be bothered. Said I was making life hard on the kids by goin' back to court all the time. What they really meant was that I was making life tough on them. Finally they warned me I might get less time with the children if I kept fighting. So I gave up."

Marj looked down, her shoulders slumping, as she toed a rut in the yard with her sandal. Belatedly she stepped on the cigarette that had long ago gone out.

"How much do you see your children now?" I asked.

"I don't," she said, still looking down, her voice a whisper.

"Not at all?"

She shook her head slowly. "Got so it hurt too much. Not just having so little time with them. Larry starting trying to turn them against me before the divorce, and he never let up after he got them. And that woman he married—"

"That self-righteous bitch," said Bert.

"—she started in on 'em too. It got so the kids didn't want to see me anymore. They had to—the courts did that much, at least—but it got so every weekend was a struggle. I could see I'd lost them—nothin' I tried seemed to work—and then I started feeling real sick. I wasn't really up to seeing them a lot of the time and . . . I don't know. When Larry wanted to move with the kids to Modesto, there didn't seem to be any point in saying no."

Marj gave a small shrug and pressed her eyes shut. When Bert asked, "Hey, hon, you all right?" she didn't answer.

I said: "Bert made it sound like you hold Bauer responsible. I thought it was some other minister who gave you the trouble."

That brought her back to life. Her head snapped up, and there was anger in her eyes. "Yeah, that horrible little man did the dirty work. Ned. But it was Bauer who brought him in, turned me over to him, told the things I said. And later—when Bauer came back—he didn't do anything to stop what the others were doing to me. I think he wanted it to happen because I was such a sinner as to think God wanted me to be happy."

Her face slipped from anger, to bitterness, to pain, and back to bitterness, as if her feelings were an unstable chemical mix that couldn't be fixed in one form.

"Are you sure Bauer knew what was happening?" I asked.

"Don't defend that bastard to us," said Bert, angrily.

"I wasn't. I was just asking."

"He had to know," said Bert. "It's his church, isn't it." He turned to Marj. "You shoulda sued the son of a bitch. You shoulda sued 'em all."

"I told you I wanted to," said Marj, her voice shifting back to a nervous whine. "I told you a million times. My lawyer said we couldn't get enough evidence."

"The bastard should have to pay for what he done." Bert turned to me, gesturing toward Marj. "Look at her, man. I used to know her in high school. We weren't friends or nothin' then, but I knew her. She was a cheerleader. One of the most popular girls in school. Happy all the time. Now look at her. You see can she's sick. He did that to her. He ought to pay." He paused, thinking something over, his eyes narrowing. "You seen Bauer, I guess, huh?"

"Yes."

"He must be hurtin' pretty bad, huh?"

"Yes."

"That's good," he said, with no satisfaction in his face. "But it's not enough. It's not enough."

$\triangledown$

Chapter 17

THE DAY-CARE CENTER SEEMED lifeless this Saturday afternoon, save for the cartoon animals that circled it in pointless parade. Mrs. Tate, as she answered the door, looked rather pointless herself, against the backdrop of that empty children's world.

"Mr. Strickland," she said. "Is something wrong?"

"No. I just wanted to talk. Is it a bad time?"

"I'm not exactly dressed for guests," she said, touching the old flowered housedress she was wearing. "It's my day to be cleaning lady."

"I think you look fine."

She laughed, not with coyness, but as if she found the compliment totally absurd. Yet I meant it. Mrs. Tate had a pink-cheeked Scandinavian prettiness about her that didn't require much in the way of artifice. The shabby housedress even gave her a kind of homey appeal. And there was a dignity about this woman that would have been evident in any clothes and in any situation.

Mrs. Tate motioned me inside and led me through the empty playrooms. We went to the kitchen, sidestepping a Hoover vacuum cleaner and a plastic pail full of cleaning supplies. On the kitchen table with its yellow plastic cover were a tea pot and cup and a small plate covered with pastry crumbs. I declined an offer of tea, and we both sat down.

"Is there any news?" she asked. When I hesitated, she added: "I know about the ransom note. Vernon told me. He said it was supposed to be confidential. But he felt I had a right to know."

She seemed to wait for me to challenge that. I said: "He's got the right to that decision. Anyway, with the church board and others in on it, it's going to be leaking out soon enough."

"Have the kidnappers started collecting the ransom?"

"Yes."

"Have they . . . ?" She leaned toward me, then pulled back. "There's so much I want to ask. But I don't know if I should. I don't want to be unfair and put you on the spot."

"There's no danger of that. The police aren't letting me in on much at the moment. As a matter of fact, I was just on my way over to see Reverend Bauer. I was hoping the police told him more than they're telling me. You might call him later yourself."

"I might do that," she said, in a noncommittal tone. "What was it you wanted to talk to me about?"

"I wanted to warn you to be careful."

She frowned. "About what?"

"People know about you and Reverend Bauer."

The shock in her face was as severe as if I'd just committed an obscene act. Her body recoiled from me.

"I don't know what you're talking about," she said angrily.

"I think you do. Someone saw you two together at a motel in Porterville."

Her lips began to form another denial, but she gave it up. Other responses were formed and got inhibited, causing her face to bloat with frustration. Finally her face went cold.

"It was certainly kind of you to pass along this gossip," she said, in a disgusted tone. She stood up. "Now that you have, I'd like you to get out of my house."

I got up from my chair and started to go. But I didn't think she'd be able to leave it at that. It's hard to turn away someone who holds your deep secret without finding out what he intends to do with it.

"You can hardly expect me to believe that you brought me that piece of dirt as a friend, can you?" she called after me.

I turned. She was standing by the table, gripping the top of a chair back with both hands, tightly, like someone clinging to the side of a life raft.

"Maybe not," I said. "But I didn't bring it as an enemy either."

My conciliatory tone just seemed to embolden her, though the boldness didn't run deep. I could see tears shimmering below the surface of her anger.

"You love to pry, don't you," she said. "You're a snoop, a dirty snoop, and you just love to get your hands on people's dirty secrets."

"Yes," I said. "When the secrets might have something to do with saving a child's life."

She looked at me as if I'd just started speaking Romanian. "What on earth are you talking about?"

"Look at it from my side," I said. "I'm hired to find a boy who's disappeared. Now I find out that the boy's father—a married minister—is having an affair with the woman who took care of his son. Wouldn't you want to know more if you were in my place?"

"Do you really think that *I* . . . ?"

"No," I said. "Though I'd be a fool if I felt absolutely certain of anything like that. But how do I know there isn't, say, some boyfriend in the picture who hates the man and figures he can hurt him—hurt the woman too, maybe—by hurting the child. Plus pick up some easy money while he's at it."

"There isn't any *boyfriend*," she said, indignantly, emphasizing the word as if it, particularly, had offended her.

"But I wouldn't know that unless I checked."

She rattled the chair in frustration. "Why did you have to be so devious? Why didn't you just come out and ask me?"

"Maybe I should have. But would you have reacted any differently if I had?"

She thought for a moment, tugging at a thick strand of hair as if she were trying to pull out a conclusion with it.

"No." She tugged some more. "No, I guess not." The anger stayed in her face, but it was joined by something like resignation. She let out a deep breath. "Sit down. I'll talk to you." She glanced around the kitchen. "First I'm going to make up some of that coffee I just bought. This is going to be a lousy visit. I want to get at least something good out of it."

She went to the drainboard and began working. She filled a coffee press with grounds and boiling water, then pushed down on the plunger with the fierceness of someone trying to detonate an explosive.

A couple of minutes later she came back to the table carrying a tray with two cups of coffee, a cream pitcher, and a sugar bowl. She put the unasked-for cup of coffee down in front of me with an aggressive rattle, daring me to decline her hospitality. I didn't, and the coffee was very good.

She sat for a few moments, sipping her coffee, perhaps asserting herself by making me wait. Gradually her eyes grew reflective, and her facial muscles visibly relaxed.

"It's true," she said, softly. "What you heard. About Vernon and me."

She was turned to the side, looking out the window. Her eyes had an intensely focused look, as if memories were taking shape against the empty landscape.

"At least, it was true," she said. "It's over now. It's been over for several weeks. It didn't last long. A couple of weeks at the most. Vernon was feeling so guilty. I felt guilty too, but I love him so much I . . ."

She stopped, sucking in her breath. Her eyes began to moisten, but she shook her head once, hard, telling herself no. Her tone became flatter with the effort at control. She said: "I guess I've been in love with Vernon for a long time. I just didn't want to admit it. I told myself it was respect, friendship, admiration—all the lofty things. It wasn't lofty at all, but I kept trying to delude myself that it was. Even when the two of us began to spend more time together because of Billy."

She sighed. "You shouldn't blame Vernon. Everything just hit him one night. We were here. Just the two of us. Talking about Billy. Vernon broke down and started to cry like a child. My heart went out to him so—this man who'd been such a comfort to so many people. I wanted to comfort him, to . . ." She paused and her face went stern for a moment. "Tell the truth," she said, as if to the part of herself that had just been speaking. "What it was, was I wanted him. I loved him and I wanted him. I should have stopped it. I should have been the strong one. It was my fault. He's a good man."

"Why be so hard on yourself?" I said. "It's absurd to take all the blame."

She gave no sign that she'd heard me. But after a moment, whether coincidentally or not, her face softened a little.

"It was all sort of ridiculous," she said. "Here we were, two middle-aged people of some experience, acting like two young kids who'd just made love for the first time. What we mostly did afterwards was talk about how guilty we felt, how scared we were of getting caught. There was so much talk, and so little of anything else. It was so ridiculous. And so . . . lovely . . ."

An almost inaudible whimper came from deep inside her, and her eyes suddenly reddened. But she clamped down at once, every facial muscle taut, holding it back. In a way it was more touching than tears would have been, the desolation visible beneath the control.

Apparently as a distraction, she reached for her coffee cup, rushing the drinking a little so that she made a slurping sound, splashing some liquid onto the outside of her mouth. She laughed at herself, embarrassed, the act of laughter spilling out a few drops of moisture from her eyes. She grabbed a napkin, dabbed at her mouth, then made a surreptitious swipe across her eyes before putting it down.

"Maybe we were a little like kids," she said. "You get away from . . . you know . . . physical love for a while, and you lose your sophistication pretty fast. I hadn't been with anybody in that way since my husband died. I thought that was just fine. Vernon told me that he and Martha haven't had a physical relationship for some time. He says she's not a very physical person. He didn't say that to blame her. He admires her spirituality so much, and he feels that abstinence is suitable to their ages. He was really blaming himself for all the desire he still had. Anyway he had it. We both did. The two of us were like an explosion waiting to happen. A very brief explosion," she added, with laugh that seemed to hurt.

She turned toward me with a little look of surprise. "Why am I telling you all this?"

"Maybe it's a relief to tell someone," I said. "Anyone."

She shrugged. "Maybe it's a way of humiliating myself. I seem to have accomplished that just fine." She took a deep breath. "To answer your question—if I haven't answered it already—no, I don't have a boyfriend. I've only had a few dates since my husband died, and they were some time ago. They were all very proper and very boring, and I'm sure the men were just as relieved as I was when they were over. I don't know of anyone besides Vernon who is even remotely interested in me in the way you mean." She laughed, this time with some real humor. "I believe that's what's called a negative confession."

The humor lasted only a moment. Her face turned solemn, then took on a look of disgust. "Vernon and I have certainly been great witnesses for Christ, haven't we," she said. "But please, don't judge the Lord by the weaknesses of His children."

"I don't know. If I judged the Lord by you and Reverend Bauer, I think He'd come out pretty well."

She looked at me with genuine bewilderment. "You must have pretty low standards," she said, with enough of a smile to show me that she was insulting herself, not me.

"Pretty high, I think. But different from those of your religion. I put a premium on kindness. You and Bauer both strike me as kind people."

"Was it kind of us to cheat on Martha?" she asked, determined to be her own inquisitor if no one else would.

"I don't say what you were doing was right. But it's only part of what you are."

"You're generous," she said, her face softening. "But if either of us is kind, that's the Lord's doing. It's His kindness showing through in us."

I shook my head hard. "Your God is lots of things. Kind isn't one of them."

"But He *is*. He's loving—infinitely loving."

"You'd never know it from looking at the world He made."

Mrs. Tate sat up in her chair, leaning toward me. The attack on her God seemed to have roused her from the doldrums of self-accusation.

"I know there's a lot of awfulness in this world," she said. "But that's man's doing, not God's."

"I don't think God should get off the hook that easily. I know the argument: God's children rebelled of their own free will, and God, being just, had to punish them. But think about it. Would you throw your own children out of Eden into a world like this one? To die of leukemia, maybe, or be burned in a fire? To be committed for schizophrenia, or suffer from Tourette's and depression like Billy? A friend of mine once said that if we treated our children the way God treats His, we'd be arrested for child abuse."

I expected her to get angry, but she only looked sad. She nodded, though I couldn't imagine at what.

"The world can be a terrible place," she said. "When people turn to Christians to ask why, we give them such heartless answers. We tell them, you've got leukemia because some relative of yours thousands of years ago offended God and God's paying him back." She gave a little shudder. "We try to dress it up, of course, but that's what it comes to. I can't believe I used to accept answers like that. I'm afraid I don't think much of Christians who do. I wonder where their minds are. Even more their hearts. How someone can see people suffering so—children suffering, above all—and settle the question with such stupid answers is beyond me. The kindest thing I can think about such people is that they are just burying their feelings to avoid despair." She shook her head slowly, almost reluctantly. "I don't have an answer to why there's such suffering. I frankly don't see why a loving God would have created a world like this one."

I looked at her with bewilderment. "Then how can you be a Christian?"

"Because I know Christ," she said. "I feel His love. He's the most loving Being I can imagine. Experiencing the Lord like that, I can't believe He could do anything cruel or wrong. There's got to be an answer to why there's suffering in this world. Do you see what I mean? If you loved someone you experienced as kind and there was circumstantial evidence that they had committed a crime, you wouldn't believe they'd done it—would you? You'd have to go with what you knew about them."

"I suppose so," I said. "But then I'd assume you could pin the crime on someone else. Who could you pin this world on but God? And why would God make Himself look so guilty? Why would He make believing so difficult?"

"I want to say maybe it's to test us. But that would seem heartless too. The fact is I don't know why. I just know there must be a reason."

I shook my head in frustration. "You run into a belief that looks absurd so you say it's a test. But maybe it isn't a test. Maybe it's just absurd."

"Maybe," she said. "But if it were a matter of certainty, they wouldn't call it faith, would they? Anyway, what's the alternative? Are you so happy looking at the suffering in the world and thinking that it's totally without purpose? That it's never to be redeemed?"

"No."

"I don't think I could live believing like you do."

"You could," I said, with a smile. "You just might not like it much."

But she didn't want to be distracted by humor. "You told me last time that you used to think of yourself as a Christian," she said. "Did you mean a born-again Christian?"

"Yes."

"So you felt like you had a personal relationship with Jesus?"

"Yes."

"Then you must understand something of what I'm talking about."

"Yes," I said. And after a moment: "Oh, yes."

I knew what it meant, all right, that personal relationship with Jesus. To a young boy, it had meant always having that voice inside you, the voice that came from beyond the stars to speak words of consolation in tones as soft as a young girl's. It meant having a friend who would listen endlessly to your hurts and hopes. It meant lots of love. Though never unconditional love.

There were so many dos and don'ts. More than that there was a fundamental repudiation of everything temporal, physical, human. "Lay not up for yourselves treasures upon earth, where moth and rust doth corrupt, and where thieves break through and steal. But lay up for yourselves treasures in heaven. . . . For where your treasure is, there will your heart be also."

This world is not my home, I'm just 'a passin' through
If heaven's not my home, then Lord what will I do
The angels beckon me from heaven's open door
And I can't feel at home in this world anymore.

I was born again in sixth grade. I'd been running away from Christian witnesses for two years, and I thought I was gaining on them. What I didn't know was that they were laying back by then, looking beyond me for some disaster to smack me down and show me my need for the Lord. It came soon enough: a schoolyard paper-clip fight, a scratch across a girl's cornea, agonizing weeks of wondering whether I had blinded her. While my father fussed over the liability insurance, my mother moved in like the Hound of Heaven. I knew what salvation would cost, and I held out as long as I could. But I had more guilt than I could carry, and I knew no other way to get rid of it. So I gave in and gave myself to Jesus.

It did cost. It meant no dancing, no parties, no sexuality (however incipient), no high spirits, no rebelliousness. It meant always being required to step forth and proclaim your beliefs, no matter how much of an idiot it made you feel—playing the fool for God. What it really cost was the one thing a teenager fears more than anything: isolation from the crowd—instant loneliness.

I think of the years that followed as a kind of delirium. The lonelier I became, the more I threw myself into Bible reading and prayer and witnessing for Jesus, into fantasies of leading world crusades for Christ or being martyred in some heathen land in His name. I remember myself sitting by my open window at night, staring up at the dark sky, praying. "Oh, Heavenly Father, take my life and make it over into what You want it to be. Bend my will to Yours, make me an instrument of Your love, so I can say with Paul, not I, but Christ in me." In my attempts at total submission, I felt, for the first time in my life, loved. At the same time, quietly and indirectly, but as surely as any Muslim fanatic, I was dreaming of death.

The fever broke sometime late in high school, broke like an abscess of its own excess, as loneliness, anger, and just plain puberty came bursting through the skin. The energy burned itself out in a two-year orgy of sex, alcohol, and orneriness. When it was over, I didn't go back to my old religious ways. I was out, and I wanted to stay out, to live a life of some normalcy. But I kept believing even as I stopped practicing, and the contradiction nagged at me in the quiet hours of my life. Occasionally I would hear God's words to the Laodiceans. "Thou art neither warm nor cold: I will spew thee out of my mouth."

It was ten years before I came back. By then I had reached the point that any older adult knows, when youthful excess has turned to what feels like pure hangover, when peace in the soul stops being a synonym for boredom, when some feeling of goodness becomes a necessity rather than a burden. The point came for me when a relationship gone bad had left me feeling worthless, and an investigation gone bad had almost left me dead. After walking the streets one night, I went into an empty church and bowed my head.

The Lord I gave my heart to this time seemed gentler somehow, less demanding, less obsessed with dos and don'ts. No doubt that was a reflection of the church I'd stumbled into, a church of Christians who took their faith as a gift to be marveled at, not as an instrument of self-mutilation or as a weapon to be used against others. My years there were a time of peace and healing. It was there too that I met Katie. She seemed like an incredible reward from God . . . until she was taken away.

I told all this to Mrs. Tate, who let me know she had heard from Bauer about the death of my wife and baby. Mrs. Tate was a good listener, keeping her eyes on mine as I spoke, occasionally asking a question but mostly just making sounds of acknowledgment or sympathy.

After I'd finished speaking, she said: "It's hard for me to imagine someone feeling that close to the Lord, then turning away from Him. But from what you said your faith started in anger. It certainly ended there. Maybe that's it. "She looked at me for a moment. "I wish there was something I could say that could help you get around that anger and back to Him."

"Yeah," I said. "Sometimes I do too."

$\triangledown$

Chapter 18

MEMORIES OF THE PREVIOUS night with Charlie grew more vivid the closer I got to her house, as if I were taking a short drive through time.

Her room had been small and dark, but the feeling I retained was of brightness and space, walls crumbling to let in sunlight and air. There'd been so much letting down, letting go, and letting in. We'd started with tentative touches and whispers, moved to passion and confession, and ended with the laughter of the children in the adults at play. It had been a special time, and I knew that whatever might happen with Charlie and me, last night would be one of those memories my mind would conjure up whenever I asked myself what had mattered in my life.

Charlie's house appeared—the real house, in real time—and I pulled to the curb. As I got out of the car, I saw Julie coming down the street on her bicycle. She was hunched forward, pedaling furiously, her red-ribboned ponytail flying behind her like a pennant. She was racing two boys, straining to stay just ahead of them. Suddenly she raised her hand in a victory salute and gave herself a cheer, having passed the finish line. As she slowed, the boys went by her, leaning back to make derogatory remarks in disgruntled losers' tones.

Julie caught sight of me, waved, and coasted back. She

stopped in front of me, straddling her bike, legs angled to the pavement like two kickstands.

"Hey, Dave!"

"Hey, kiddo. You look pretty slick on that bike. You weren't too rough on those boys, were you?"

"Naw," she said, giving me her tomboy grin. "Not too rough."

"You were pretty rough on me at Crazy Eights the other day."

"Sorry about that," she said, cheerily.

"Yea, well, you just wait, Big Shot," I said, pointing at her like a cop threatening a crook. "Next time we play, *you're* doin' the dishes."

"No way, José," she said, in a miniature tough guy voice, cracking me up.

Julie was wearing denim shorts and a white boy's shirt with the ends tied across her bare, tanned midriff. It was an ageless sort of outfit. If I squinted a little, I could see her as a teenager or even a young woman, see her growing up before my eyes like the boy in the old Wonder bread commercial. I hoped her growing up would be good.

"Whatcha doin'?" she asked.

"Going to the Bauers' house. Thought I'd say hi to your Mom first. Is she home?"

"Nope. But if you keep goin' where you're goin', you might just find what you're lookin' for."

It took me a second to get Julie's joke. "You mean she's at the Bauers'?"

"Yep."

"Why?"

"I don't know. Something about answering the phone."

"I guess I better go ask her." I took a step away, then stopped, not wanting to just shuffle Julie aside. "Hey, kiddo, walk me over there, will you? It'll give us another minute to visit."

"Okay." Julie hopped off her bike and began walking it alongside me, limping a little in her brace.

"How's your summer been going?" I asked.

"Bor-ing."

"How come?"

"Theresa's away. She's my best friend."

"You must have other friends around here."

"At school. Not here."

"What about those boys you were racing?"

"Gimme a break," said Julie, looking at me as if I were crazy.

"So . . . where'd Theresa go?"

"To the mountains. With her mom and dad. They got a cabin there, and a boat, and they go swimming and fishing and everything. They took me once, for a weekend." Julie's eyes lit up, as memory took the place of envy. "It was *really* neat."

We came to the Bauers' gate. Julie left her bike on the sidewalk and came through the gate with me.

"You catch any fish when you went?" I asked.

"Oh, man," said Julie. "I got one this big." Julie held her hands out a ridiculous distance apart.

"How about we go fishing some time?"

Her eyes widened. "You mean it?"

"Yeah."

"When?"

"Soon. When my job's done."

Julie's face turned solemn. "You mean, when Billy's back."

"Yeah."

"Maybe Billy could come fishing with us."

"Maybe. If his parents stop hugging him long enough to let him."

Julie laughed. We were on the Bauers' porch now, by the front door.

"I better go in," I said.

"Okay. See ya." Julie clumped down the porch steps, then turned back. "Hey, thanks." She glanced toward one of the Bauers' windows, off to the side of me, and waved. "Hi, Mom!"

In a moment Charlie opened the door. She was dressed

mother/daughter style today—denim shorts, white shirt, even a red-ribboned ponytail—though her shirt tails were discreetly tucked in, perhaps because she was at the Bauers'.

I couldn't quite bring Charlie into focus, and then I understood why. She wasn't just red hair and freckles and cuteness anymore. She was now the tastes, scents, and feel of her against me when we made love; the giggles and playfulness of the naked pillow fight she'd started in the middle of the night; the tears and the secrets she'd let me share. It was as if I was suddenly seeing her in four or five dimensions, instead of three.

I started to grin when I saw her, then felt the grin fall away. Charlie wasn't grinning; she wasn't even smiling. Her face was all closed up, almost angry looking. I started to take the look personally, but knew that couldn't be right, not after last night. It had to be something else.

"Charlie, is something wrong with the Bauers? Where are they?"

"They're down at the lake. Holding some kind of service."

"Bauer told me he was getting a substitute."

"He couldn't."

"I'm surprised he didn't call off the service."

"Maybe he just got sick of sitting around here worrying," said Charlie, an edge of antagonism in her voice, as if we were opponents in an argument.

"Charlie, if the Bauers are all right, then what's wrong? It's obvious something is."

She glared at me as if in confirmation.

"Charlie . . . ?"

"What were you saying to Julie just now?"

"What?" I asked, totally off balance.

"What were you saying about fishing?"

"You heard that?"

"What were you saying?" she insisted.

"I said maybe I'd take her fishing. What's the big deal? You're mad about that?"

"You didn't say maybe. You said you would. For your information, that is a big deal. Especially to a seven-year-old."

"Charlie, what I said just now was a slip of the tongue. Yes, I told Julie I'd take her."

"But you were thinkin' maybe you wouldn't."

"No, Charlie, I was thinking I definitely would. When I tell someone I'm going to do something, I do it."

"That's real big of you. What were you going to do after that? After you'd gotten all her hopes up?"

"Charlie, what in hell are you talking about?"

"What were you planning for a follow-up, huh?"

"I don't . . . ?"

"You gonna pop into our lives, sweep us off our feet, have us live happily ever after?"

In reflex response, I took half a step back. Charlie looked down at my feet with an angry, triumphant look.

"Yeah," she said. "That's what I thought."

I wanted to kick myself for my reaction. And maybe Charlie for hers. "Come on, Charlie . . . you know I . . . but we just . . ."

"Exactly," said Charlie, as if I'd actually said anything. "In a little while you go and we stay. And that's fine with me. We've been through a mess, Julie and me. We're finally getting clear. I've got the custody thing behind me, and I've almost got my degree, and there's going to be a good job waiting for me, and we're going to be okay. I don't need any hassles. I don't need anyone pressing me."

"Charlie, you're not making any sense. First you say I'm not committing myself, then you say I'm pressing you."

"I don't have to make any goddam sense if I don't want to!"

I looked at her with my mouth open. It was a point in an argument when both people should burst out laughing at the absurdity of it. But I could tell that Charlie wasn't about to laugh and that I'd better not either. Still, something had to give. Charlie gave a sigh and put her hands up in a half-hearted gesture of concession.

"Look, I know I'm not making any sense," she said, over-enunciating the way people do when they're making an effort to control their tone. "I'm really pissed off, and I don't know why, and I'm just not in the mood to figure it out right now. So just don't push me to make any sense."

"Okay, but . . . Charlie, I just don't get it. Last night was so great . . . you said so too . . . this is the last thing . . ."

"I said I didn't want to talk about it!"

Charlie's hand shot out toward the front door, to shut it. I put a hand out to stop it.

"Charlie . . . wait . . . please . . . just a second. I'm not going to press you. I'm going to go now. I need to talk to Bauer, and I'm going to try to catch him at the end of that service. I'll call you later. Maybe you'll feel like talking then."

"Maybe," she said, her face softening a little.

"Charlie, you don't have to respond to this. I just want you to know how really special I thought last night was."

"It was nice," she agreed, but sadly, as she pushed the door shut. "Too nice."

I stared at the closed door, shaking my head and muttering "women." I didn't know if I was being clutched at or run away from, and worse, I didn't know what I wanted. I kept running over it in mind as I walked away from the Bauer house, getting somewhere with my feet, but nowhere with my head. By the time I gave the subject up, I was deep in the woods. I heard voices and slowed my pace, not wishing to disturb them.

Ahead, through the trees, I could see the baptismal service. There were about fifty people standing on the shore of the inlet, most of them dressed in the sports clothing that serves as dress-up in summer in small towns—the men in subdued short-sleeved sports shirts and pressed cotton slacks, the women in bright shirt-and-skirt outfits. They were watching the baptisms with affectionate reverence—except the children, who scampered about the water's edge, obviously delighted by the spectacle of adults dunking each other fully clothed.

Reverend Bauer, Mrs. Bauer, and a heavy blond woman were standing out in the water, waist deep, wearing the black baptismal robes I remembered from childhood, the kind with weights sewn in the hem to keep the skirt of the robe from floating. Bauer put his right arm around the blond woman's back and with his other hand placed a white handkerchief over her nose and mouth. He tilted her backward into the water "in the name of the Father, Son, and Holy Spirit"—a maneuver that resembled a dance dip by two stiff, overweight dancers. The woman came up spluttering in spite of the handkerchief, but laughed good-naturedly, while those on the shore cried "hallelujah" and "praise the Lord." The woman was given a small towel by Mrs. Bauer to mop her face and hair, then waded to shore.

Four of the people on the shore were dressed in robes—all dry—so it was obvious that the baptisms had just begun. I sat down on a tree stump to wait, glancing around at the woods. I hadn't appreciated the beauty of the place the other day, having been absorbed in the case and irritated by the heat. Now it was much cooler, more so than the early evening would account for. Glancing up, I saw some wisps of cloud in what had been a sky of hazy blue monotony. Perhaps we were in for a change of weather.

A teenage boy was the next to be baptized. As I watched him, my mind drifted back to my own baptism in the small pool that lay beneath the podium of the church I'd attended with my mother after my conversion. I had gone through the service full of fantasies of the great deeds I would one day do for God, of the baptisms I would someday conduct, perhaps along some African river, for the poor benighted natives I had brought to Christ.

I remembered standing in the warm baptismal pool, the pastor's arm around my back, the handkerchief over my nose, remembered being tilted backward into the chlorine-scented water that would wash away all my sins. Of course, baptism was not really the moment of salvation, only the profession and symbol of it—of the death of the old, lost, sinful self. "Therefore we are buried with him by baptism unto death . . . that the body of sin might be destroyed . . . For he that is dead is freed from sin."

As my mind drifted back and forth between present and past, my eyes kept picking up and letting go of the elderly woman who was now stepping out into the waters of the inlet. I saw her initial expression of excited anticipation; her look of uncertainty as she realized she'd moved too soon and was in the path of the teenage boy who was coming to shore, toweling off, not seeing her; her awkward, tentative moves as she half-splashed herself out of the boy's way into the slightly deeper water; the lurch of her body as she stumbled over something and almost fell; her fright as she discovered that first her foot, then the hand she reached under the water with, were caught.

All my attention was on the woman now as I watched her panicked struggle to free her arm, heard her call for help to Bauer, who was splashing his way toward her.

Suddenly the woman's arm broke the surface, and she began to scream. There was a hand on her hand, a terrible purple, bloated thing, holding on as if trying to pull her down. Or as if beseeching her for help.

It was the hand of a child.

$\triangledown$

Chapter 19

THE SIGHT OF BAUER lifting that body from the water wouldn't leave my mind, even hours afterwards, as I sat alone in my motel room.

The body had been his son's, but barely recognizable, something out of a nightmare. Bauer had stood holding the body in a paralysis of horror, like a man being electrocuted who's powerless to let go of the wire that's killing him. Finally I'd splashed my way out into the inlet and wrenched the body out of Bauer's arms. Then he'd begun to sob.

I knew that the dead boy's face and Bauer's sobs weren't going to leave my mind any time soon if I stayed there in my motel room. I was trying to decide between running and drinking when the phone rang. I reached for it with desperate relief.

"Dave?"

"Charlie. God, it's good to hear your voice."

"Are you all right?

"Yes. It's just been a horrible evening."

"Poor Billy. It makes me sick."

"Me too. He's been dead this whole time. The police think the kidnappers killed him Monday right after they took him. Held him under the water to drown him, then submerged his body in the lake."

153

Some rocks had been stuffed into the dead boy's clothing to sink his body, and the submerged body had become tangled in vines. It was the vines the elderly woman had gotten caught in that had created the illusion of the hand grabbing her.

"Why would they kill him, Dave? What would be the point?"

"I don't know why. All I know is what they did. Charlie, it was just awful today. What the Bauers must have gone through . . ."

"That's why I'm calling. Wayne just phoned me—I'm home tonight with Julie. Someone at the bar told Wayne he'd seen Reverend Bauer in a bar a little while ago—drinking pretty hard."

"Oh, shit. What bar?"

"The Carousel. It's a little place on Main Street—about a block from the movie theater."

"In his emotional state he may be pretty hard to stop—especially if he's been drinking awhile. But I'll try."

"I don't understand him. I know he's hurting a lot and I know he must want a drink real bad, but how can he leave his wife alone at a time like this?"

"She may not know the difference. She was really out of it the last time I saw her. It was strange. Most of the people at the lake were getting pretty hysterical, but Mrs. Bauer—there was nothing from her at all—not a scream, not a tear, not anything. She just sort of . . . disappeared inside herself. She was like a robot or something. She may be in the hospital by now."

"The poor woman. I don't even want to think about how it'd feel to find your child like that."

"I know." I glanced at my watch. It was past midnight. "If I'm going after Bauer, I'd better go now."

"Yes. Go. I just want to apologize for today. Last night was really special for me too. I guess I got scared."

"That's all right. I'm scared too. Maybe it would be easier if we got scared together. How about if I come by in the morning and we talk about it?"

"I can't in the morning. I've got to open for Wayne tomorrow. I traded with Louise so I could be home with Julie tonight. I'll be home about five."

"I'll come by then. How's Julie?"

"She was pretty upset—crying most of the evening. She's finally asleep now. I'm going to go curl up with her as soon as I get off the phone."

"I'm sorry she's hurting."

"Before we found out about Billy, she was going on about your taking her fishing. She was really excited about it."

"You don't mind?"

"No, I think it's great. But look—don't let me keep talking. Go see if you can find Reverend Bauer."

"Okay. Good night, Charlie."

"Night, Dave."

I hung up the phone and went outside. Downtown was only a couple of blocks away, but I took the car in case I needed it to transport Bauer. I drove to Main Street, passing a Mid-Cal bank, with its lighted, deserted ATM machine in front. I knew that as of two hours ago, Wernecke was stalling on a cancel order for the stolen ATM cards—still hoping for that elusive ATM photo. I'd suggested he get the bank to program the ATMs to eat the kidnappers' cards in case they were used again—then check any card he got for prints. I didn't know if he'd take me up on the suggestion; I wasn't sure I really cared. Billy was dead, and the case was over for me. The rest was up to the cops, and nothing they could do would bring that sad little boy back to life.

I drove past the movie theater, then spotted the Carousel bar, which occupied a narrow frontage between a cleaner's and a pharmacy. The exterior was all brick and dark glass, making it inconspicuous from outside and private within. It looked like the kind of place that would attract weekday drinkers from the local businesses, not a place that would have much happening on a weekend evening.

I parked and went inside. The place wasn't much bigger than a train car. The left wall was all mirrors and bottles, with a bar that extended out a third the width of the room. The rest of the width was a narrow walking aisle and a few tables squeezed against the other wall. The place was dimly lit from a few colored bar lights and jukebox and a Ms Pac-Man video game.

I'd been right about the place being quiet on a Saturday night. Ten customers, mostly older and alone, didn't make for much excitement. Unless the only excitement you wanted was alcohol.

Bauer was sitting against the wall at the end of the bar nearest the door. There was no one seated near him. I walked over and climbed onto the bar stool next to him.

"Evening, Reverend."

He gave me the drunk's slow turn. There was something like hostility in his red eyes, but it was sluggish and muted, like something viewed under water. There was nothing incongruous about seeing the minister in that bar, since I knew his past. In fact, he looked like he was home, the gnarled and splotched face come back to the source of its shaping. The hand that held the beer glass—there were two shot glasses of whiskey nearby—was scarred along the knuckles. Something about being in a bar setting made me notice how really big he was.

I wasn't sure how I was going to play it until I sat down. Bauer didn't look like he was in any frame of mind to listen to lectures about demon rum. It was going to take something indirect. The first thing to do was to get him out of there.

I ordered a draft beer, waited in silence while it came, took a sip, then waited until the bartender moved off.

"I'm sorry about your boy," I said. "Really sorry. What you went through today must have been hell."

Bauer glanced my way briefly, the hostility replaced by surprise, and then pain. His lower lip quivered, and he bit down on it to make it stop. He turned away and took a long pull on his beer. Then he tipped one of the shot glasses back and drained it.

"I got drunk as hell the night my wife died," I said, which was not quite true—it had been four days afterwards. "Kills the pain some, and that's good. Feels like you're killing yourself some, and that feels good too. Don't know why, but it does."

Bauer didn't give any acknowledgment of having heard. He just kept drinking.

"Felt like absolute hell the next day," I said. "That was good too. When your body hurts enough, you almost forget for a little while the other thing that hurts so much. Not for long, but for a little while."

I took another sip of beer. "I got drunk a bunch of other times," I said. "Drunk, hung over, drunk, hung over. I got no regrets. Got me through it."

I was silent for a few moments, as we sat there, drinking together. "Did one stupid thing though," I said. "I got rowdy a few times—told myself it was all in fun, but there was a lot of mean underneath it—know what I'm saying? You must, from the old days. Got in a few fights, cops were called one time, I took 'em on." The sour laugh I gave came out sounding staged to my ears, but Bauer was unlikely to be making any fine discriminations. "Got arrested and came close to losing my license and my living over that one. At the time I didn't give a shit. Later, of course, I did. Hadn't'a been for a couple of friends intervening, I would have lost it. As it was I got suspended for six months. Funny: It's so hard to care at the time. Later there's too much time."

I wasn't lying exactly, more like embellishing. I would have gotten arrested if one of the cops called in hadn't been someone I'd once worked with on the force, who'd heard about my wife. Instead of taking me in, he'd taken me back to my place where he'd sat on me until he could sober me up enough to read me the riot act. I owe him a lot.

"You, Reverend, you don't have to go picking a fight with a cop. All you need to do is keep sitting right where you're sitting. Word will get around. The folks at the church will hear all about it. Maybe you'll be lucky like I was and only get a small reprimand or suspension. But after that story you gave me about Marj Hempell, I somehow doubt it.

"Not that you give a shit. No reason you should. Problem is you will later. Even if you don't, there's the matter of your wife. From what I saw today, she's going to need a lot of taking care of—and a normal life to get back to. Your getting canned from the church won't help a hell of a lot on either count."

I watched him as I spoke. Toward the end I thought I saw his drinking arm hesitate just a moment as it moved upward, but that may have been wishful thinking.

"Got a proposition for you," I said. "I got a quart of Jack Daniels in my motel room. Easy to get more if that's not enough. Or something else if you want. Got a car right outside. We could drive back to my motel. Sit down in my room and have some drinks. You want me to leave, I leave. You want the room to yourself all night, you got it. I can find someplace else to stay. Tomorrow, you decide you want to stagger out on Main Street and give everyone the finger, you can go ahead and do it. At least you'll have had the night to think on it."

If he didn't go for it, I didn't know what else I could do, short of trying to cold-cock him and drag him out of there. For what seemed like several minutes, nothing happened. Then he started to get up off the stool. He maneuvered with the drunk's exaggerated care, getting a foot caught once in the rung of the stool and almost pitching backward, but catching himself. He lumbered out the door, and I followed.

I drove him back to the motel and helped him out of the car. Fortunately, we could get to the room without having to go through the lobby. I took Bauer across the dark parking lot toward one of the side entrances, taking child-sized steps as he made his slow, clumsy progress.

Bauer and I entered into an empty lighted hallway next to my room. He stood aside as I unlocked the door, then stumbled ahead of me into the room. He didn't sit. Immediately his eyes started searching the room.

"Where is it?" he said, thickly, the first words I'd heard out of him.

I closed the door, putting on the chain. The chain would be a minor obstacle to someone inside, even someone drunk, but it would give me a few extra seconds if I needed them.

I took a deep breath. "Reverend, if you were anyone else, I'd say, go ahead, get as drunk as you like. I should probably say that anyway. But for some goddam reason I care about you. You're an alcoholic. You said that the last time you fell off the wagon, it almost killed you. I can't let you drink anymore. Sorry I had to trick you. It just seemed better than the other options."

Bauer was staring at me with a puzzled look; it seemed to be taking his brain a few extra seconds to absorb the message. I knew when he got it, he wouldn't like it. Once again I became aware of how big he was.

"Reverend, why am I getting the feeling that this is going to hurt me more than it hurts you?"

The joke was for me, since Bauer wasn't exactly in the mood for humor and anyway not much was going to get through to him in his condition. Glaring now, Bauer began to march straight at me as if I and the door behind me simply didn't exist.

"Don't try it, Reverend Bauer," I said.

He pulled up a couple of steps in front of me, glowering, his eyes red as if from fury, though I knew most of that was from the alcohol.

"Move," he said.

I shook my head.

"Move."

I shook my head again.

He swung. I was ready for it and in his drunkenness he'd telegraphed it. But even at that he was fairly fast and very strong. Although there was almost no body behind his punch, my arm still went numb when I blocked it. With the other hand I reached out and pushed him in the chest. He stumbled back a step or two, almost fell, but recovered.

"Don't, Reverend."

He came charging at me. He started to throw a laughably obvious right, and only at the last second did I realize it was a fake, that it was the left coming. I dodged and only partly escaped. His left fist glanced off the side of my head, making things fuzzy just for a moment. As a reflex, I threw a fist straight out, felt it connect with soft flesh, heard a painful exhalation of air, and heard him hit the floor a moment later.

As my head cleared, I saw Bauer sitting on the floor against the wall. He was twisted to the side, vomiting on himself and the rug. I went into the bathroom, wetted one towel and grabbed another dry. I came back, waited until Bauer finished vomiting, then started cleaning him up.

"Bastard," he said. "You son of a bitch." His words had a slurred anger to them, but the rest of him lay limp and unprotesting.

"Yes," I said, finishing up on him and starting to work on the rug.

"Why can't you . . . leave me alone?"

"Because I don't want you to die."

"Don't care if I die," he said. "Don't care about anything."

"I know," I said. "I know."

And he began to cry.

Chapter 20

I WOKE FACING THE window and the thickening clouds—gray on white on blue. Over the mix of colors were splotches of black, as if someone had defaced the sky.

The digital clock by the bed read 10:00 A.M. I looked toward the place on the floor where Bauer had been sleeping when I'd finally fallen asleep at 5:00 A.M. The pillow and the blanket were on the floor, but Bauer was gone.

There was no point in chasing him. I couldn't baby-sit him forever, and if he was bent on self-destruction, he'd manage it in spite of my efforts. He'd been given a forced respite to think about it. The rest was up to him.

Still, as I showered and shaved, I began to get curious about him. After I'd had coffee and doughnuts in the motel dining room, I drove out to Bauer's house through the quiet Sunday streets.

No one answered the door after several rings, so I went around back. Mrs. Bauer was there, seated in a rocking chair. She facing my direction, and I waved. She made no sound or movement. I saw that her expression didn't change, and her eyes didn't seem to focus.

An elderly woman, wearing a nurse's uniform, came limping down the Bauers' back steps. She saw me and came over to the fence.

"You the one ringing the front door bell?" she asked.

"Yes," I said.

She gave me a reprimanding look, as if I were some young rascal playing tricks on her.

"I rang it four times," I said. "No one answered."

"I don't move as fast as I used to," she said, looking at me as if that were somehow my fault too. "Besides, I got a patient to look after."

"How is she?" I asked, nodding toward Mrs. Bauer.

The old nurse just shook her head.

"Is she in shock?" I asked.

"Could be. Is there something you wanted?"

"I came to check on Reverend Bauer. Is he home?"

"He was, a little while ago. He changed his clothes and went over to the church. Insists he's going to give the sermon."

"You're kidding."

"I don't kid much," she said, matter-of-factly. "I told him it was ridiculous, no one would expect it. Told him it would be unseemly. But he insisted." She shrugged with the resigned look of one used to having her advice ignored.

I walked over to the church, the sound of hymn-singing growing louder as I approached the front door. I entered the vestibule. A solitary usher gestured me to an empty place in a back pew of the nearly full church.

There was no sign of Bauer. The only person on the pulpit was a young man, who was leading the congregational singing with the exaggerated hand gestures of a trained music director. When the hymn was over, the young man spoke to the congregation. He said they must all be aware of the sad death of the pastor's son and would understand that the Reverend Bauer would not be speaking today. Instead there would be a short service of Bible reading, prayer, and hymn-singing dedicated to the pastor and his family. He asked the congregation to pray that the Lord would be with Reverend and Mrs. Bauer and grant them His love and strength in full abundance.

I was getting up to leave when Bauer walked through a door at the side of the pulpit. A murmur started at the front of the congregation and rippled out through the room until the whole congregation was full of sound. The young man looked around for the source of the noise. When he saw Bauer he made a gesture of surprise, then rushed over to the minister. There was a brief conversation in which the young man's body language seemed both solicitous and dissuading, Bauer's resolute and a little impatient. When it was over, the young man took a seat at the rear of the platform and Bauer went to the lectern.

He looked acceptable. He'd changed into a clean dark suit, white shirt, dark tie. His hair was combed, and his eyes looked all right, at least from my distance. I'd watched him carefully as he'd walked across the platform, and I was convinced he wasn't intoxicated. But there was something contracted and awkward about him—perhaps from jitters not quite under control.

Bauer coughed softly to clear his throat, tried to speak, then coughed twice more. The congregation was now absolutely silent in that way crowds only get when they've been shocked into it.

"I don't want to be here today," said Bauer, in a voice that was still badly hoarse in spite of all the throat clearing. "Billy is dead, and Martha is very sick, and I don't want to be here. But I've got to be. There are some things I have to say."

Bauer kept shifting position as if he couldn't get comfortable. His hands kept regripping the sides of the lectern.

"What happened to Billy made me hate God," said Bauer.

He looked around at the congregation. People around me began shifting uncomfortably in their seats.

"The police say the people who took Billy for money killed him right after they took him," said Bauer. "Killed him out of pure meanness, probably. The police say they took my boy to the lake, grabbed him by the hair, and held him under the wa—"

The last sound came out as a kind of verbal shudder, a sob barely contained. Bauer looked down for a moment, fighting for control. When he started speaking his voice was pitched slightly higher, as if it had ridden up on tears that had gotten closer to the surface.

"—held him under the water until he drowned. And the God who sees every sparrow that falls watched my son being murdered and didn't raise a hand to help him."

Just in front of me a small girl let out a sob. The woman who put an arm on the girl to comfort her didn't seem to be breathing quite right. All over the congregation people were looking toward the pulpit with a frightened expectancy, as if believing something terrible and irreversible was about to be said.

"All of you know that I used to be a drunk before I found the Lord. Last night I started drinking again. I knew it was wrong, and I didn't care. I wanted to keep drinking until I couldn't feel the pain anymore. I knew it could kill me, and I didn't care about that either.

"A friend stopped me from drinking. He tricked me into going with him to a room where there was no alcohol. And I, a minister of God, tried to hurt him so I could get out of there and get more to drink. It was a disgrace, but such were the depths of my despair.

"He hit me, and I fell down, and then I got sick. I began to cry for my boy, and then I fell asleep. When I woke the sun was just up and the man was sleeping. I woke angry—angry at him, angry at the world, and most of all angry at God. I wanted to get out of there and start drinking again, but I knew it was too early to get a drink, and anyway I felt so sick I couldn't move. As I lay there, sick in body and sick at heart, smelling the stench of filth on my clothes, I seemed to hear the words of Job's wife, who told Job to curse God and die. That's what I wanted—to curse God and die."

Bauer looked slowly around his very uncomfortable congregation. His anger had given him an aggressive stance at the lectern, shoulders hunched forward, neck stretched forward, eyes glaring. Someone not knowing the context might have taken him for a thug threatening these people.

"Then the Lord began to speak to me, and I said, 'No, I don't want to hear your words anymore. I don't want to hear how everything we are and have is yours, and how you give and take away at your pleasure. You shouldn't have taken

my son. I don't want your words. I want my son back. And
don't talk to me about your love. You gave my son a miserable
life and a miserable death. What kind of love is that?'

"And the Lord said, 'I know your pain,' and I said, 'No,
you don't. You sit up there in the clouds where all is joy and
peace, and you move us around like pawns on a chessboard.
You don't know what it's like, the pain and the despair we
feel. It's all just a theory to you. Whatever it is you think
you're doing, it's not worth the death of my son.' "

"For a time all was quiet, and I thought, finally, I have
driven Him away. But then His voice came again, softer, so
soft I could barely hear it at first. He said, 'I had a son. I
loved him more than anything. He was a good and beautiful
boy. In the morning of the world I would hear His laughter
ring through the heavens, and it made me happy.

" 'But somewhere in the world I had other children, and
they were not so good. They had broken the laws of the
universe, and they were going to suffer eternal death for that
unless someone died in their place. The only one who could
die for them was my Son. You complain that I watched while
those men drowned your boy. But did I not also watch while
my Son was spat on, and mocked, and nailed to a cross? How
can you say I don't know your pain? You say you're not
willing to accept the death of your son as a price for the divine
plan. How can that be—when you were so willing to accept
the death of my Son?'

"When the Lord stopped speaking, my heart was still hard
against him, and I said, 'But your Son is there with you, and
my son is dead.' And He said, 'You fool, don't you know Billy
is here with me now . . .' "

Bauer's voice broke, and he gave a deep, wrenching sob.
His face became a terrible grimace of self-control, keeping
back more sobs, though not the tears.

" '. . . he's here with me now, in the arms of my Son. He
doesn't shake anymore, and nor does he utter those terrible
words that came from his brain against his will. No one here
is afraid of him or makes fun of him. His depression is gone.
You say I did not lift a finger to help him when those men

killed him, but you are wrong; he is my child as much as yours, and I was with him to give him strength and comfort. His pain was brief, and his memory of it is gone, and he will never have to suffer again. He holds no bitterness against me because he sees now how things are, and how the dark and light fit together, and why there had to be pain. Just as you shall see one day when you embrace your son again.' "

Another sob came from Bauer, and he lowered his head, his shoulders shaking, crying silently. After a few moments he looked up.

"My son is dead, and I don't want to be here today. But the Lord told me to come. To tell you of my despair and my joy. To tell you again that He loves you, loved you enough to send His only begotten son to die for you, so that you might live forever with Him. To tell you not to despair for Billy because he is safe, nor for me and Martha, for the Lord will give us the strength we need until He takes us home."

▽

Chapter 21

I WAS THE FIRST one out of the sanctuary at the end of the service. Two deacons were positioning themselves at the front doors of the church for the usual handshaking and conversation, but I moved by them fast enough to discourage either. I noticed that one of the men was Warren Hadley.

Outside, as I crossed the lawn, I saw Bauer emerge from a back door of the church, apparently slipping away just as I was. I went after him, jogging a little to catch up with his long, quick strides.

"Reverend Bauer," I called. As I caught up to him, I said: "I came over this morning to see how you were. I heard your sermon in there. I guess that means you're okay."

But even as I spoke, I saw that something was wrong. I was expecting a peaceful, reconciled man. The man in front of me was all tension and jitters.

"You are okay, aren't you?" I asked.

"I don't know," said Bauer. He was shifting feet, gripping and regripping one hand with the other. "I feel angry . . . and all keyed up . . . like something terrible's going to happen. I don't know why. Maybe it's the effects of the drinking."

"Or the shock. You're bound to be feeling that for a while. But after what you said in there, I'm sure you'll be fine."

"I believe what I said in there," said Bauer, as if I'd challenged him somehow. "I've got to."

Bauer turned abruptly and hurried away. I stared after him, wondering about him, hoping he was going to be all right.

As I trailed behind Bauer, heading for my car, I saw a patrol car cruise by and stop just down the street. Wernecke and a sergeant got out, then walked toward the crowd of people now gathered outside the church. I went back to see what was going on.

By the time I reached the police officers, they were escorting Warren Hadley off to the side, out of earshot of the other churchgoers. The sergeant noticed me approaching and started to run me off, but Wernecke signalled him no.

"What's all this about?" demanded Hadley of the police officers.

"Do you know where we could find your son?" asked Wernecke.

"Certainly not in church," said Hadley, with a disgusted look. "I assume he's at home in bed. What's—?"

"He's not home. None of his friends seem to know where he is."

"If they don't, I certainly don't."

"What about your daughter?"

"Sharon? What's she—? Look, I'm not answering any more questions until you tell me what this is all about."

Wernecke stared at Hadley for a moment. His face was masklike, but I thought I saw a flash of pity in his eyes. "Mr. Hadley, your son is wanted in connection with the kidnap-murder of Billy Bauer."

"No!" The word came out of Hadley like a cry of pain. "No! Jim's kind of wild, and we've had our disagreements, but he'd never do anything like that. You're wrong. I know you're wrong."

"I don't think so," said Wernecke, patiently. "Last night we got ahold of one of the auto-teller cards that the kidnappers were using. There were fingerprints on the cards. When we ran the prints through ALPS, we found—"

"Through what?" said Hadley, sounding slightly dazed.

"Automated Latent Print System. It's a computerized fingerprint identification system. The prints on the auto-teller card matched the prints from your son's service file. We talked to the man who owned the stolen card. He doesn't know your son. He can't think of any reason why your son's prints should be on that card."

"There's got to be some mistake," said Hadley. "I just know there's an explanation. Maybe . . . my son was in the same store with the man and—"

"There hasn't been any mistake," said Wernecke, interrupting, the patience gone from his voice. "This morning one of my officers tried to apprehend your son. Your son pulled a gun on the officer and took a hostage."

"Dear God," said Hadley.

"Who's the hostage?" I asked.

"A young woman," said Wernecke. "Benton. Char—"

"No!"

I must have blanked out for a fraction of a second because the next thing I knew, I was gripping one of Wernecke's suit lapels, and the sergeant was yanking my hand away.

"Strickland, what the hell's wrong with you?" Wernecke was saying.

"Not Charlie!"

"You know her?" asked Wernecke. Something changed in his eyes. "Sorry. I didn't know."

"Tell me," I said. "What the hell happened?"

Wernecke grimaced. "A bunch of bad breaks. The ID on the prints didn't come through until after the bar closed. By the time we went looking for Hadley, he was nowhere to be found. We don't know where he spent the night, but this morning, for some reason, he went to the bar. Dawson spotted him going in." Wernecke gave a small sigh. "Unfortunately she went in alone—and without calling in first. Hadley pulled a gun and took the Benton woman hostage. Holding the gun on Benton, he forced Dawson into the back room and locked her in. When Dawson broke out, she called us."

"What about Sharon?" asked Hadley. "Surely you don't think she's . . . ?"

"We don't know that she's involved," said Wernecke. "At the moment we just want to ask her some questions. But we can't find her either."

"You have any idea which way they're headed?" I asked.

"No," said Wernecke. "But we got an APB out on them. Someone will spot them."

"Has anyone been sent to take care of Charlie's daughter?"

Wernecke glanced at the sergeant, who just shrugged.

"I better do it then," I said.

I walked toward the street, feeling sick about Charlie, sick about what I had to tell Julie. I kept looking for that familiar little figure on the bicycle, but she was nowhere in sight. As I started up the walk of Charlie's house, I saw a young Hispanic woman eyeing me from the yard next door where she was watering some plants.

"Mrs. Benton's not home," said the woman.

"I know. Is Julie here?"

"I'm watching her today. You come back when Mrs. Benton is here."

I walked over to the woman, showed her my investigator's license, and told her what had happened to Charlie. As I talked, she kept glancing at the police car parked at the church, seeming to find confirmation in my words in the sight of that vehicle. When I'd finished, and she was through with her exclamations and questions, I told her I needed to tell Julie. She nodded solemnly and gestured for me to follow her.

As we approached the front door, I heard the television blaring cartoon noises. I followed the woman, Mrs. Alvarez, inside. Julie was sitting on the floor of the living room in front of the TV, wearing a gray-and-pink cotton nightgown and slippers that looked like two gray elephant puppets. When she saw me, she gave me a big grin.

"Hey, Dave!"

Seeing how happy she looked made the idea of telling her all that much worse. I swallowed hard.

"Hey, kiddo."

"Mom's not here right now."

"I know. Let me turn that off, okay. There's something I need to talk to you about."

Something in my expression seemed to alert Julie. Worry showed in her face, but tentatively, like something she hoped she wouldn't need. Her eyes searched my face, trying to read there exactly what I was going to tell her.

I walked over to the television set. The screen showed creatures getting clobbered, bouncing around, then emerging unhurt—the best of all possible worlds, perhaps. But not ours. I shut off the set.

When I turned, Julie was staring at me. She looked close to weeping.

"Is there something wrong with my mom?" she asked, in a voice that wasn't quite all there.

I put my hands out in a calming gesture. "Your mom isn't hurt, Julie. Believe me, she isn't hurt. But she is in trouble. Why don't we sit down?"

"What kind of trouble?" demanded Julie, not moving.

I sat on the edge of one of the couch cushions and gestured toward the cushion next to me. Julie just shook her head.

"Julie, do you know what a hostage is?"

"Yes," she said, as a reflex. Then: "No, I'm not sure."

"You know how on television, when one of the bad guys is about to get caught, he grabs an innocent person and points a gun at the person, so the police won't dare come near him."

"That's what happened to my mom?" asked Julie, in frightened disbelief.

"Yes, but it's not as bad as it sounds at first. Think about it. If the guy hurts the hostage, what's to keep the police from grabbing him? He's got to keep her safe."

But the reassurance I was trying to give wasn't working. Julie was still in the process of absorbing the awfulness of what had happened. She stood in front of me, her face scrunched up as if she were about to sob, her head swinging from side to side as if she were looking for escape.

"Julie, I know you're feeling scared. But it'll be all right. Really. Come over here, will you?"

I put out my arms to her, but she shook her head. I dropped my arms, feeling stupid and more than a little inadequate. I gave Mrs. Alvarez a helpless look, then turned back to Julie.

"Hey, kiddo, I know I'm not doing this very well," I said, hearing a quiver in my own voice. "But I know how much you love your mom. I care about her too. I'll do everything I can to get her back safe. Everything. I promise."

Julie ran over to me then, throwing her arms around my neck and leaning her head on my shoulder, letting me hold her while she sobbed. Holding her, I felt such a helpless rage. I'd meant what I'd said about doing everything I could to get her mother back safe, but I knew there might be nothing I could do, knew, in fact, that it might already be too late.

When Julie's tears had subsided, and she'd-gotten some hugs from Mrs. Alvarez, she began to talk, struggling toward a little optimism, latching onto what I'd said about hostage takers not wanting to hurt their hostages. Even though I couldn't share the optimism I was trying to give her, just seeing her brighten a little made me feel better.

Julie helped me call her grandmother and break the news and arrange for Julie to stay over there. While Julie went to her bedroom to pack, I researched the separate addresses of Jim and Sharon Hadley, using a phone book and a town map that Charlie kept with some other odds and ends on the counter by the kitchen phone. When Julie was ready, I drove her to her grandmother's. I talked to the woman for a few minutes, then gave Julie a big hug and left.

As I drove away, I began to think about Charlie in the hands of the kind of people who had no compunction about killing a five-year-old boy. I knew such thoughts could get me crazy, rob me of my ability to function. So I tried to close off the feeling parts of my mind, narrowing myself down to the focus necessary to proceed. Find where they'd gone. That's all there was. Find where they'd gone—whatever it took.

It was just a few minutes to Jim Hadley's place, a small duplex in town. As soon as I saw the two patrol cars parked in front of it, I knew that I wasn't going to get any closer than a glimpse from the street. I could only hope that if there was something there to find, the police would find it.

It took me almost forty-five minutes to locate Sharon's place, which was several miles outside of town, and not quite where I had thought it would be from the map. It was a small ranch consisting of a large stable and corral, and a shack of a house.

There were no patrol cars, and no visible neighbors. I knew from my conversation with Sharon that she was divorced, but I didn't know about roommates. I knocked on the door, then peered through windows, to make sure there was no one inside. Then I began searching for a way in.

Circling the house, I found a small bathroom window designed like a pair of cupboard doors latched from the inside. There was some give in the windows, and I worked them back and forth until the latch flipped up and the windows swung outward. I wriggled my way through the opening and down into the bathtub, supporting my descent with the shower fixture, the curtain rod, and the built-in soap dish.

The inside of the house consisted of a living room, kitchen/dinette, two small bedrooms, and one hall bath. The living room had a set of newish western furniture and prints that might have been ordered whole from the Montgomery Ward's catalog. The furnishings in the other rooms could have been dumped off by a Salvation Army truck.

I went through the house slowly, starting with the bedrooms, one of which had been given over to storage. I kept my eyes open for any obvious evidence that Sharon had been involved in the kidnapping, but that wasn't my main purpose, and I could hardly take any such evidence to the police. If I found any, I'd have to leave it where it was and make an anonymous phone call.

What I really cared about now was some indication of where Hadley might have gone with Charlie. Most of my search focused on the kitchen where Sharon kept her phone,

phone book, bills, records and receipts. Her phone was a pushbutton with redial, so I went to my car and got out of the trunk a small tape recorder and a RadioShack acoustic coupler. Back in the house I put the suction mike on the phone receiver and plugged the jack into the tape recorder. I turned on the tape recorder and pushed the phone's redial button. The pulse tones played their melody, and the phone rang at the other end, but there was no answer. I put my tape recorder away and got out my Polaroid, taking photos of every page in Sharon's small phone book. I also took a photo of what looked like a bill for mortgage payments on some sort of property in Porterville. There was nothing else, so I left.

As I drove back to town, I thought about how I was going to reach my phone company contact in San Jose on a Sunday. Then suddenly I remembered the bartender's sullen reach-out-and-touch-someone joke. I turned toward Henry Tuttle's house.

He answered the door in jeans and a plaid sport shirt, a bandage still on his cheek. His face, seen through the screen door, didn't look happy to see me. His mother was bustling somewhere inside, and he kept glancing nervously over his shoulder, as if I were a disreputable friend he didn't want her to see. He spoke in a near whisper.

"What do you want?"

"You're a technician at the phone company, right?"

"Yes," he said, but tentatively, as if reserving the right to change his answer.

"I need your help. I've got a recording of some pulse tones. I need you to run it through one of those test sets at the phone company and get the number for me. And then look up the address that goes with it."

"You know I can't do that."

"Yes, you can. Tuttle, it's important. The police found out who killed the Bauer boy. The man—"

"What?" Tuttle's face pressed eagerly against the mesh of the door for an instant, distorting its features. "They know who did it?"

"Yes."

Relief lit up Tuttle's face. "Who was it?"

"Jim Hadley—a singer at one of the bars in town. He's taken a hostage, a woman I care a lot about. There's an outside chance the phone number I want may help me figure out where they went."

"And get me in trouble—maybe cost me my job."

"No way. What we're doing has nothing to do with evidence. How I got the number shouldn't ever come up. If it does, I'll make up some story. I'll keep you out of it—I promise."

Tuttle just stared at me. I felt my temper flare.

"God damn it, Tuttle, you owe me. Anything happened to my friend because you didn't help, I'd never forgive you. You've got to help. Don't make me get nasty. God damn it, please."

My voice had gotten pretty loud. Tuttle was madly making shushing sounds behind the screen door.

"Henry," his mother called, sharply, "what's going on out there?"

"It's all right, Mother," he called back, soothingly. "Just a little problem at work. I'll be back in an hour."

Tuttle slipped out the door like a little kid escaping for an hour of play—except that the irritated look he gave me told me I wasn't the companion he wanted. He didn't speak until we were parked in front of the phone company, when he insisted on going in alone. I handed over the tape and watched him disappear inside the building.

I sat waiting for about fifteen minutes. My eyes were half-closed and I was lost in thought, so I almost missed seeing the car. If it'd been any color other than orange, it probably wouldn't have registered at all. When I did see it, the VW was two blocks away, just turning a corner. I started my car and took off after it.

I caught up to the VW on the highway outside of town. As I pulled alongside, I could see that a clean-cut young man was driving. I honked and gestured him to the side of the road. When he hesitated, I pulled my wallet out and held it open, as if I were showing him something official. He nodded and pulled his car to the shoulder. I parked just in front of him, wrote down the license number, then got out and walked back. He remained in the car, like someone waiting for a parking ticket. As I approached, I watched his hands, which stayed on the steering wheel.

"I'm a private detective working with the Azalea police," I told him, as I leaned toward the driver's window. "They've been—"

"I just talked to them, sir," said the young man. He was about college age and had a preppy look. He was wearing a green Izod sports shirt and khaki trousers.

"To whom? The police?"

"Yes, sir. I've been up in Mendocino all week visiting a friend from college, and I just got back. I heard about the police looking for a car like mine, and I went into the station just now. Nobody seemed all that interested. They asked me who I was and what I was doing at the Bauer house, and then they said I could leave."

"What were you doing at the Bauer house?"

"I was there doing my summer job. I work for the Gospel Press in Fresno. We sell Bibles and other Christian books door to door. Mrs. Bauer had bought from me before, so I went back to see if she wanted anything."

"What time did you get there?"

"About five. Maybe a little after. I think that's about right because I remember thinking that it was going to be my last call."

"And you didn't see anybody hanging around outside the house?"

"No, sir."

"Well, thanks. Sorry if I startled you."

"That's okay."

I started to move away, then turned back. "Did Mrs. Bauer buy anything?"

"No, sir. I never saw her."

"She didn't come to the door?"

"No. I figured she wasn't home."

"Did you check around back?"

"Yes. There was no one there either."

"Maybe she was in the bathroom."

"Maybe. But I waited quite a while."

"Okay. Thanks again."

I drove back to the phone company. As I pulled into the same parking spot, I could see Tuttle standing just inside the hazy glass of the door. He rushed out, looking as furtive as a cat burglar.

"Where were you?" he asked, irritably, as he slid into the passenger seat.

"Sorry. An emergency came up. You have any luck?"

"I got your number," said Tuttle, shoving a typewritten sheet of paper at me along with the cassette. "And the address. Mountain Reality. Pine Lake. It's just above us in the mountains."

I felt a surge of excitement. I knew it might be nothing, but it was a chance, and I allowed myself a little hope.

"This is great, Henry. Thanks a lot—I mean it. I'm sorry I got so pushy back there. I was feeling a little desperate."

Tuttle's face softened. "It's okay. You were right; I did owe you one." He nodded toward the paper in my hand. "You think that'll be any help?"

"God, I hope so."

$\triangledown$

Chapter 22

T HE MOUNTAIN ROAD CURVED like a carnival ride through
a labyrinth of trees. The car jerked and slid as I pressed the
accelerator, frantic for speed.

The car skidded on gravel, and I eased up, reminding myself that I wouldn't be any good to Charlie wrapped around
a tree. I didn't want to remind myself that I might not be
any good to her anyway—that I might be in the wrong place,
or just plain too late.

The road continued to curve and climb. Gradually the
trees began to thin out with the higher altitude; the road
leveled and straightened. There was a deserted ski resort, its
lift suspended motionless above the boulder-strewn ground.
Then some cabins, with a group of children playing on a
nearby outcrop of rock. Then a lake, its surface dotted with
sails, its edges shaved of vegetation, reservoir style.

Finally I came to the town of Pine Lake, a group of cabiny
buildings lining the narrow two-lane highway. The place
looked as primitive as the Old West until you saw the signs
on the buildings—offering everything from frozen yogurt to
physical therapy.

I found Mountain Reality at the far end of town. A hand-
written sign on the door said, "Back at 3:15," which meant
I had twenty minutes. I used the time to gas up the car and

get a takeout order of sandwiches and milk. Then I parked in front of the realty office to wait, eating my lunch in the front seat of the car.

I was crumpling up the sandwich wrappings when a tan Ford sedan pulled up next to me. The man who got out of the car was balding and middle-aged, wearing dress slacks and a flannel shirt. He glanced my way with a salesman's all-purpose smile, then unlocked his office door and went in. I got out of the car and followed.

Inside the office, the man introduced himself as Carl Baty and welcomed me to Mountain Realty. When I told him I was a private investigator, his welcome cooled considerably. His eyes began twitching as if he were doing some quick calculations—perhaps adding up the peccadilloes of his life, wondering if someone was finally sending him a bill. When I told him I was assisting the Azalea police in tracking down a fugitive, he looked enormously relieved. I said: "Mr. Baty, there's reason to believe that the man we're after phoned your office yesterday or today. If so, he may have rented something from you. His name's Jim Hadley, though I doubt he'd have used that name. Early thirties, five-ten, dark hair, full beard if he still has it. Have you dealt with anyone who fits that description?"

Baty shook his head firmly. "No. No one like that."

"Maybe his sister then. Late twenties, but looks younger. Five-foot, slender, has sort of a pixie cut." Baty looked hesitant, and I added: "Name's Sharon Hadley. Or . . ." It took me a second to remember her married name. "Sharon Dean."

The expression on Baty's face told me I'd hit it right. I felt a surge of hope and adrenaline so strong it almost knocked me off balance. I shifted feet and sucked in my breath. Baty was saying: " . . . rented to Mrs. Dean this morning. But I don't understand. She seemed so nice. You say she's done something wrong?"

"Her brother has. She may be helping him. What'd she rent?"

"The Morrison cabin. It's a couple of miles from here. Said she had friends joining her."

"What time was that? When she was in the office, I mean."

"About ten."

"Then the others have probably joined her by now."

I told Baty enough about the situation to get him nervously excited about cooperating. He gave me directions to the Morrison place, described the property in some detail, and agreed to wait for the police. Then I called the Azalea police and gave directions to the realty office, adding directions to the cabin in case something happened to Baty. I told the sergeant on the other end of the phone that I was heading out to the cabin now, then hung up when he started yelling at me to stay the hell away from there.

A few minutes later I was driving north out of Pine Lake. I set the trip odometer to zero and watched the tenths of a mile roll by. When the odometer said two miles, I watched for a clearing with a huge boulder and a sign that said "Danger: Climbing Prohibited." A short distance beyond that was the mailbox I was looking for, the name on it weathered almost beyond recognition. I slowed as I passed the narrow dirt driveway, but everything beyond the first curve was hidden behind pine trees and brush. I drove a tenth of a mile past the mailbox and pulled over to the side of the road.

I got out and opened the trunk. I pulled out a shoulder holster and got it strapped on beneath my jacket. I took out the Colt detective special, loaded it, and put it in the holster. Then I walked into the woods. I knew from what Baty had told me that the Morrison place was surrounded by state lands, so I wasn't going to have to worry about stumbling onto some other citizen's property.

After pushing my way through the thick underbrush for a couple of minutes, I saw the house to my left, through the pine trees, about a hundred yards away. It was a single-story cabin, elevated over a three-foot-high open space where wood was stacked. At the front of the house, the dirt driveway ended in a circular parking area. Two vehicles were parked there, a blue pickup and a yellow station wagon. Behind the house was a clearing with a small, windowless storage shack.

Behind the shack the land dipped away into an immense wooded valley.

As I stood there, the front door of the cabin opened and Sharon came down the front steps and went over to the station wagon. Behind her, the cabin door opened again, and her brother stuck his head out, calling something to her I couldn't catch. She acknowledged with a wave, rummaged around inside the car for a moment, then emerged with a grocery bag and some clothing that she carried back to the house.

I was suddenly conscious of my heart pounding. Up until this moment, the chase had been almost theoretical. Now it was real.

It hit me that since leaving the realty office I'd been running more on frantic energy than logic. It was time to think this through, to decide what I should do.

I was convinced that if Charlie was alive, she was here. I had to assume that she was alive and do whatever gave her the best chance of staying that way. The cops might care about Hadley, but I didn't give a damn about him. All I wanted was Charlie—safe.

The ex-cop in me told me to wait for reinforcements. I knew how that would go: the cops surrounding the place at a distance, using the bullhorn, negotiating, waiting, trying to talk Hadley out. If Hadley had been a simple bank robber, that approach would have made sense. But the kidnap-murderer of a five-year-old boy might not be real motivated to surrender himself and his hostage. And though the police would be concerned for Charlie's safety, they wanted Hadley, and they'd only let themselves be jerked around so far. I understood that in principle—but not where Charlie was concerned.

On the other hand, if I went in by myself, I could blunder and spook Hadley. He might be more likely to kill Charlie in a moment of panic than if he sat around and thought about it, knowing he was trapped.

I finally decided to move in cautiously, looking for a chance. If it came, I'd take it. If it didn't, I'd leave the whole thing to the police.

What held me was the thought of that unguarded driveway. According to Baty, it was the only possible way to get a car out of there. I didn't want to risk these people driving away while I was in the woods. Again it wasn't a matter of Hadley. I was convinced that the farther away they were and the longer they had Charlie, the worse her chances would be.

After thinking about it a moment, I went back to my car and parked lengthwise across the narrow dirt driveway at a spot where there'd be no way of getting around it. It might screw up the cops a little bit, but it was worth the risk, and I could always move it for them later.

I walked back into the woods and considered how I was going to get close to the house. The trees weren't dense enough to hide me standing up. The underbrush was thick enough to hide me crawling, but then what? I wouldn't be able to see anything stretched out on the ground in the middle of all that vegetation. And the underbrush had been cut away within ten feet of the house, making it dangerous to maneuver close to it.

As I thought about it, my eyes kept fixing on the open area under the house. If I could get under there, perhaps I could hear enough to know who was in the house and where. If any of them emerged, I could come at them from an angle they would never anticipate. It would be an unpleasant place to be if I got caught in a cross fire between Hadley and the police, but a cross fire seemed unlikely in a hostage situation, and anyway, there was the stacked wood for cover. The first real difficulty would be covering the ten feet of open ground between the brush and the house. But it was worth a closer look.

I checked myself over. Most of what I was wearing was brown and beige; only the paisley tie, with maroon in it, would stand out. I took it off and slid it under a bush. I mentally charted a path through the bushes, then got down on my hands and knees and began crawling.

I moved a little bit at a time, testing every point of contact with the ground for noise, taking care not to cause movement in the larger vegetation. It took me about twenty minutes to get just short of the point at which the underbrush had been cut back.

I lay very still for a time, listening, half decided that moving farther was a stupid risk. Then I heard a woman's voice somewhere in the cabin—not Charlie's, Sharon's maybe—and heard a toilet flush—on my side, but toward the back—and without consciously thinking about what that might mean, I slithered my way across the open space. Under the house, I lay still again, trying to hear over my panting breaths and my thudding heart. In a moment I heard the woman's voice again, and then the man's, sounding normal enough, and decided I'd made it.

I looked over my hiding place. The underside of the house was at least three feet high—plenty high enough to allow me to move on hands and knees. There were stacks of fire logs and kindling along the front and back, and old planks in the center, but I could maneuver through the entire area if necessary. Doing it quietly would be another thing, however, since there was debris over most of the dirt surface. I began slowly clearing an area that ran front to back on the side I had entered.

That done, I spent some time listening. What I wanted most of all was simple reassurance that Charlie was here. But I also needed to know where she was. And I needed to know if the Hadleys had any other partners here with them. I suspected not, since there were only two cars, and Sharon had come to the realty office alone, and I doubted if Hadley would have tried to pick up an associate on the run. Still, it was possible that someone else was here. And I had to know.

For a time there were no sounds at all. Then I heard what seemed like that same woman's voice again. Then silence. Then a conversation between a man and a woman. Then silence. After a time I became fairly certain that the Hadleys didn't have any partners here with them. But I also began to get the terrible feeling that Charlie wasn't here either. And not here meant dead.

Don't think like that, I told myself. She's here, she's got to be here.

I continued to wait and listen under the house, knowing that time was getting short, knowing that the police had to be getting closer. What I was hoping for was for both the Hadleys to step outside—not unthinkable if Charlie was tied up. I could take them both then, away from the house and the hostage. But I figured that was luckier than I was going to get. Failing that, if I could be sure at some moment that the brother and sister were both at the front or back of the house, I could try going in the other way. But it was too big a risk without knowing where they had Charlie. Come on, I kept thinking, say something, Charlie. Let me know you're there.

Suddenly the front screen door slammed shut, and I heard footsteps moving across the porch and down the steps. I slithered quickly to the front of the house, slipping behind a pile of logs. Looking out I could see a woman's denim-covered legs heading toward the yellow station wagon. I risked a better look and saw that it was Sharon Hadley.

I moved back a little, took my gun out, and waited, tensed. Come on, Hadley, I whispered. Come outside, you bastard.

I heard the car start. My first thought was that I had Hadley alone now, and then my stomach turned over as I remembered that my car was blocking the driveway. Sharon would be back in a moment, knowing someone was here. Then Hadley would know, and the element of surprise would be all gone. I had to act.

I tried to picture what would happen in the next minute. Sharon would get to the end of the driveway, see my car, and panic; there was no way she could turn her car around, so she'd simply back up, fast. She'd get out of the car and run up the porch steps, maybe yelling to her brother as she went, maybe forcing herself not to speak until she got inside.

As the yellow station wagon was pulling away, I tried to picture how Hadley would react when he heard that station wagon coming back. Even if the car's approach didn't sound frantic to him, even if he assumed his sister had simply forgotten something, he'd be on edge. He'd have to check it out, anyone would. Wherever he was, he'd move to the front of the house. And that was my moment. I'd just have to hope he didn't have Charlie near him.

I crawled fast to the back of the house, stopping just short of the small back steps. I heard the car coming back, fast, the horn sounding in panicked blasts. I love you, Charlie, I whispered, as I moved out from under the house. I hope like hell this works.

I started up the back steps, fast, but in a kind of walking stride, feet placed rather than dropped. I winced at the squeak of the screen door as I slipped inside the empty kitchen, hoping that the commotion at the front would hide the sound of the door. I moved to the kitchen entryway and slowly took a look.

I was looking down a narrow hallway that gave me a view of the center section of the living room, including the front door. Sharon was just inside the door, turned ninety degrees away from me, talking to someone who was out of sight and out of my line of fire. I cursed and pulled back. I could hear their voices now.

"What are we going to do? I'm scared, Jimmy!"

"God damn, Sis, I never wanted you involved in this. Why the hell didn't you just go home, like I told you, after you rented this place. Once she saw you . . ."

"Never *mind*," said Sharon. "Let's get out of here. Let's go out the back."

"How fucking far do you think we'll get on foot? And how do you know he's not out there in back somewhere?"

"I guess I don't. But we got to do something."

"What the hell did you see out there? Just one car? You sure?"

"That's all I saw."

"No cops?"

"I didn't see anyone."

"Then we play her like I did this morning. We show who-ever it is we've got her, and start off in the pickup. If they don't move the damn car, we ram it out of the way with the truck. They won't dare shoot. Come on, Charlie."

Into the frame of living room came a glimpse of black skirt, white blouse, and red hair, and I knew that Charlie was alive. I wanted to yell and cry and laugh, all at the same time. Instead I tightened my grip on the gun, getting ready to move.

Charlie edged into full view, her legs free, her hands tied behind her, her lower face tied with a gag. Then came Hadley, holding Charlie's right bicep with his left hand, while his right hand hung at his side, holding a gun. The three of them were grouped by the front door now, their backs to me.

Hadley was awfully close to Charlie for the shot I wanted, but I couldn't count on a better one. The thought of calling to Hadley to surrender crossed my mind, but never seriously. Any warning would give him a chance to turn his gun on Charlie, and he wasn't worth the risk to her. I took a step into the hall, aimed the gun with both hands, and fired.

In the instant of stun from recoil and noise, I realized that Hadley had taken a step to the left as I fired. I'd hit him, but not flush. The bullet hit his upper right arm, slamming it into the wall, sending the gun flying off to the right. My eyes went to Charlie first, to make sure she was all right, then to Sharon, to the left, who looked at me in shock, started to put her hands up, then suddenly dove by Charlie and out of sight, to the right, where the gun had gone.

I cursed and started for the living room, knowing I wasn't going to make it in time to keep that gun out of Sharon's hands. Suddenly Charlie took a step and, with arms still tied behind her, threw herself in the direction Sharon had gone, tilting herself to the side as she dove to protect her face. As she dove, somehow Hadley was moving too, throwing himself after Charlie.

The five or six running strides it took me to get to that living room seemed to take forever, long enough certainly for all sorts of panicked thoughts to go through my head. As I came charging around the corner, I saw three tangled bodies, and it took my eyes an instant to sort them out—Sharon on her stomach on the floor, her hand reaching out for the gun, Charlie facedown on top of her, struggling to keep the pressure of her weight on Sharon while behind her Hadley was yanking violently at her hair to get her away. The way Hadley tore at that hair set off a flash of rage in me, and it added something to the force of my foot as I kicked him in the ribs. I felt something give, and heard him scream as he fell away. Then I was on the floor, catching Sharon's hand with mine just as she got the gun, ripping her fingers away from it as she yelled, backing off her, pulling Charlie up with me as I got to my feet, one gun in my pocket, the other on the brother and sister.

"Charlie, are you all right?" I asked, then realized she couldn't talk with the gag on. I pulled the gag off with my left hand, and she started sobbing into my shoulder. I tried to soothe her as best I could while keeping my eyes and the gun on the Hadleys.

"God, I can't believe you're here," she said, when she could talk, her face still buried against my sport coat.

"Me neither. I was so damn worried. You okay?"

"Yes." I felt her face jerk up. "Julie. I . . . ?"

"She's okay. She's at your mother's. But they'll both be a lot better when they know you're safe. Is there a working phone in here?"

"In the kitchen."

"Think you can cut that rope off yourself with a kitchen knife?"

"Yes."

"Bring me the knife if you can't. As soon as you get free, phone for the cops and an ambulance. Tell them the Morrison place. After that go ahead and call your mom."

Charlie pressed herself against me for a moment in a kind of armless hug and then went off to the kitchen. In front of me, Sharon was kneeling next to her brother, patting him, whispering to him; he was curled up in a ball, a hand on his arm and side, moaning.

"How is he?" I asked.

"He's hurt real bad," said Sharon.

"There's an ambulance coming," I said. "He'll get help. He won't get much sympathy, though, not after what you two did to that boy."

Hadley's eyes snapped open, and a panic sharper than his pain flashed in his eyes.

"Oh, man, hey, wait," said Hadley. "Sharon didn't have anything to do with anything until this morning. And I didn't kill that kid."

"Who did?"

"I don't know. I didn't have nothin' to do with takin' him."

"Bullshit, Hadley. We know you were collecting the ransom."

"Yes. But I didn't take the kid. I swear it. I don't even know what happened to him."

"Hadley, save it for your lawyer. Doesn't matter what I believe. I can't do anything for you."

"But I want you to know, man. It was just a scam. I didn't take the kid. I just pretended I did, to get the money."

"Sure."

"It's true, man. I had the idea of those auto-teller cards in my head for a long time. It was just an idea—you know, like you get when you sit around watching those crime movies. I wasn't gonna do anything with it. It was just kind of a joke idea. But then Bauer's kid disappeared, and I had some people coming down hard on me for money I'd owed them—you saw what they did to Truckee—and I saw a way to pay them off and get me some money to get me out of here and give me my chance at Nashville. I never had anything to do with that kid. It was just a scam, man, just a—"

I put my hand up in a shushing gesture, as my eye caught something moving outside. Then I saw something else move, and I knew what it was.

"Cops," I said aloud, mostly to myself. "Let's see if we can get outside without getting ourselves shot." I moved toward the screen door, but to the side, out of any possible line of fire. "Wernecke," I yelled, "it's Strickland. Can you hear me?"

For almost thirty seconds there was nothing. Then I heard Wernecke's acknowledgment over the bullhorn. I yelled back: "Wernecke, it's all over. Hadley's been shot. The hostage is all right. We're coming out. Hold your fire. You hear me?"

"Yeah, I hear you," blared Wernecke's voice over the bullhorn, sounding more than a little disgruntled. And then, more quietly, like an offhand comment by an announcer who doesn't realize the mike is still on: "You fucking hot dog."

I laughed and stepped back, bumping into Charlie. I turned and looked at her. Her clothes were dirty, her hair was a mess, her make-up was gone, her face looked exhausted, and I couldn't remember seeing anything more beautiful in my entire life.

"You get Julie?" I asked.

"Yes. Everything's all right." She reached out and touched my arm. "Thank you for what you did."

"Hey, you did great yourself. I don't know what would have happened if you hadn't stopped Sharon from getting that gun. That lunge of yours was pretty gutsy."

"We make a pretty good team," she said, with a grin. "If you weren't too much of a dummy to see that."

"Me?" I started to protest, then laughed. "Yeah, I guess maybe we do."

$\triangledown$

Chapter 23

IT WAS EARLY EVENING as I drove through the empty fields. A small sign by the roadside said, "Repent: The Day of the Lord Is at Hand," while behind it dead grasses and a half-collapsed squatter's hut offered a vision of the end of the world. Far off, a tractor was throwing up thick, brown billows, as if it were reaping a harvest of dust.

Ahead of me tract houses appeared, huddled together as if against the emptiness around them. The muffled hymn I heard as I passed the church sounded like a prayer for protection. I pulled to the curb and walked to the Bauers' house.

Taped over the front bell was a note asking visitors to come to the backyard. I found the Bauers there, seated on lawn chairs. Reverend Bauer was hunched over a Bible, flipping through its pages with apparent urgency, as if searching for some answer. Mrs. Bauer was sitting stiff and still, eyes wide as if aghast, looking as if she'd found one answer too many.

I spoke Bauer's name. He looked up, put the Bible down, and rose to greet me. The dark suit coat and tie he'd worn that morning were hanging on the railing of the back steps just behind him; a mourning band encircled one of his biceps, over his white dress shirt. The desperate jitters I'd seen in him earlier seemed to be gone, buried beneath exhaustion.

"What a terrible thing . . . about Charlene," he said, concern trying to break through the weary thickness of his voice. "Is there any—?"

"She's safe," I said. "We got Hadley, and got Charlie away from him. She's had a tough time, but she wasn't hurt. I dropped her off at her mother's house a few minutes ago. She and Julie are probably still hugging each other."

Bauer tried to smile. "I'm so glad." He looked into my eyes as if trying to read something behind them. "Somebody told me they thought you and she—"

"Yes," I said.

"Then I'm doubly glad." Bauer reached out his large hand and gave me a fatherly pat on the shoulder. "I like you both a lot." He let the hand drop. "Come, sit with us. I'll get you a chair."

As Bauer walked toward a stack of folded lawn chairs, I looked again at Martha Bauer. Someone, perhaps the nurse, had dressed her in a summery white smock, brushed her brown hair to a softness I hadn't seen in it before, and put a white ribbon in her hair. With her wide eyes and taut features, the effect verged on the grotesque, as if a child had picked up a voodoo doll by mistake and dressed it up to play house.

"How is she?" I asked Bauer, as he seated me. I found myself speaking very softly, as if I were in the presence of someone sleeping, or dying.

"You don't need to whisper," said Bauer. "I'm not sure she hears us." Bauer took a slow, deep breath, as if the very effort to speak was tiring him. "If she does, that's good. The doctor wants activity around her."

"She's in shock, is she?"

"Of course."

"What does the doctor say?"

Bauer shrugged, irritated. "You know how these doctors are. You can't get them to commit themselves to anything, even the obvious."

"Shouldn't she be in a hospital?"

"That's what the doctor wanted. I didn't. I don't want her in one of those . . . places. We argued about it. Finally he

admitted it wouldn't do her any harm to be home awhile—
not if there were a nurse to look after her when I couldn't.
But he's going to insist on hospitalizing her for observation
if she doesn't respond soon."

Bauer turned to his wife and took one of her hands in his.
"Martha, you don't want to go to a hospital, do you? Talk to
me . . . please . . . just a little . . . so people will know you're
all right. Then they'll leave us alone, give us all the time we
need to grieve."

I thought I saw a slight relaxation of Mrs. Bauer's eyes.
But there was no other change. She made no sound. After a
moment Bauer gave a sigh. He patted his wife's hand and
replaced it gently in her lap.

"Did you say the police have Jim Hadley?" he asked.

"Yes. His sister too."

"Sharon? What's—you mean she's one of the kidnappers?"

"Hadley says not. At the moment it's hard to know one
way or the other. But even if he's telling the truth, she's going
to be in a lot of trouble for helping her brother."

"Poor Warren," said Bauer, his face full of pity. "He's losing
his children too." Bauer closed his eyes for a moment. "Do
they know why Jim . . . why he . . . you know . . . ?"

The words Bauer wanted seemed to stick in his throat. As
I looked at the slumping of his body, I remembered the terrible weight that grief has.

"Hadley borrowed money from some pretty rough people,"
I said. "They broke the leg of one of his band members, and
they were threatening Hadley too. I suppose that explains
the ransom. But it doesn't explain what was done to Billy."

Bauer flinched and looked away. "I wish it made me feel
better to know that the people responsible have been caught.
But it doesn't. There's no comfort in it. No comfort at all."

Bauer let his head drop into his hands, fingertips pressing
against both temples like a vise. After a time he straightened
up slowly, almost reluctantly, as if it were hardly worth the
effort.

"I'm going to fix some iced tea," he said.

"Let me do it."

"No. I need to move around a little." He stood up, clumsily, putting too much weight on the flimsy lawn chair, almost toppling over. I put a hand out to steady him. When he had his balance, he said: "I was wondering. I have a couple of phone calls to make. Would it be too much trouble to ask you to . . . you know . . . sit with Martha for a few minutes?"

"I'd be glad to."

Bauer gave me a grateful look, then turned, lumbered up the back steps, pulled opened the screen door, and went into the house. I knew how much he was hurting, and I felt my fists bunch up in sympathetic, impotent anger.

But with sympathy came memory, and I didn't want that. I forced my mind back to the thoughts that had been occupying me for much of the last two hours.

I looked at Martha Bauer, with her blank face and dazed eyes. "I wish I could see into that head of yours," I said.

I hadn't intended to speak aloud. I suppose it was like being by the bed of a comatose patient, whose presence draws out human speech while absence makes the saying safe.

"I think you know what happened to Billy," I said. "I didn't believe Hadley at first, when he said he didn't take your boy. I thought he was just trying to save his skin. But then, on my way down from the mountains today, I started thinking about you. If you were home that day, as you said you were, why didn't you answer the door to that kid from the Gospel Press? I can think of possible explanations for that, but then there was your reaction to the ransom note. Looking back, I see it wasn't just shock. What was there to be shocked about anyway, with Billy already missing five days? It was more like *disbelief*—as if you knew Billy couldn't have been kidnapped. How could you know that unless you knew what did happen to him?"

I leaned toward Mrs. Bauer as I spoke, senselessly, my body propelled by the desire to know. I stared hard at her, as if I could will her to hear me.

"What happened that day? Did you do something to Billy? Was that it? Or was it something you saw? It had to be one of the two. That's why you've left, isn't it? Why you're like this. It isn't simple grief over your child's death. I don't believe you were one to grieve like this. It's what you know. But what is that?"

I felt such frustration as I confronted her silence. There were so many questions, and I had the feeling there would never be answers.

I shifted around in my chair, turning away from Martha Bauer, staring off at the woods. There was a childish impulse in my shifting away, to cut myself off from her, as she'd cut herself off. Still I couldn't stop myself from speculating, as I stared into the thick branches of the trees.

"That day the note came, you said something about Satan being a deceiver. And . . . what else? Something about trying to make one doubt the voice of the Lord. What would that have to do with anything? Unless . . . what happened to Billy had something to do with some . . . crazy voice from God."

"Don't blaspheme, Mr. Strickland."

I almost jumped out of my chair. It wasn't just the shock of her speaking. There was something in the voice itself. It was stripped of tone and emotion, so that it sounded dead, distant, disembodied.

I swung around in my chair to look at her. There had been no change in her expression or posture. I thought for a moment I'd been hearing things. But then I noticed the eyes. They were still cold and staring, but they were focused now, on me.

"The Bible, Mr. Strickland, tells us that Christians have received 'the spirit which is of God; that we might know the things that are freely given to us of God.' There's nothing crazy about that."

"Tell me about Billy."

"Why should I?" She spoke as if from behind a mask of a face. Yet I thought I saw the barest hint of a smile at her lips.

"For whatever reason made you decide to speak to me now," I said. "And because if what happened was God's doing, you should have nothing to be ashamed of."

The barest suggestion of confusion passed over her features and then was gone. "I am not ashamed."

"Then tell me."

But she didn't speak, and after a moment I became afraid I might be losing her. I said: "You told me you checked on Billy about an hour after you got home and found him playing. Was that true?"

"Yes," she said, but there was a hint of hesitation.

"What else?"

"I saw him sneaking off into the woods."

"And?"

"I was furious, of course."

There was no hint of that anger in her monotone, nor in her body, which sat rigid in the chair, back straight, knees pressed together, hands folded together and resting in the lap of her white cotton dress.

"You followed him?"

"Yes. I couldn't move as fast as Billy could on that little dirt path. But I was patient, knowing he'd stop sooner or later. I caught up with him by the inlet. He'd stopped to watch a butterfly. He didn't know I was there until I grabbed him."

I'd been sitting absolutely still, monitoring myself for any mistake of movement or voice that might stop the flow of her words. In my hypercautious state, the creak of the porch board jarred me like the crack of a rifle shot. Out of the corner of my eye I saw Bauer standing on the steps. I was sure he was going to break in on us, stop this, and send me away. But he didn't. He looked stunned. He half sat, half fell onto the top step, holding in his arms the tray he'd brought out. Then he pushed the tray away, sliding it across the floor of the porch, toppling one of the glasses, which spilled and splintered. Martha Bauer didn't seem to notice any of it.

"Billy began to struggle," she said. "He broke free of me and stumbled back into the water. He tried to run away, across the inlet, thinking I wouldn't follow him. But he wasn't going to get away with that. I went into the water after him. And caught him."

I glanced over at Bauer. Terror was beginning to make its way through the stunned look on his face. I was struck by how very still he was sitting, like a man who's just realized that his head's been severed, who knows that the slightest movement will topple it from his shoulders.

"Billy began screaming at me. You never heard him, Mr. Strickland. You never heard the things that child would say. Filthy things—dirty, sexual things—and blasphemy against our Lord. It was terrible, there in the baptismal waters, beneath the cross. I had to stop him. I grabbed him by the hair, and I pushed him under the water, pushed him again and again, crying, 'Dear Lord, wash this filth from my son, wash him clean, make him perfect in Thy . . .' "

A deep wail came from Bauer, as if from a primitive part of himself, kept coming through the horrified mouth. Martha Bauer turned then, just slightly, enough to see him. She frowned, squinting, as if she were observing him from some great distance, as if he were too far away for her to make out who he was or what his sounds were.

"Oh, my God, Martha," cried Bauer. His face looked like something broken. "My God, what have you done?"

Martha Bauer watched with that same mild curiosity as her husband bolted inside the house. But my mind wasn't on either of them now. It was on a five-year-old boy with a Dodger cap and a chipmunk face and a brain that didn't work quite right. I could almost feel his terror as he struggled against this crazy woman—his own mother, who had given him life and should have cared for him above all things—as she shoved him down into that water again and again, determined to cleanse him of his sins at any cost. The boy's very panic would have made it impossible for him to stop his screaming, until the water filling his lungs stopped it for him, and cleansed him for good.

He that is dead is freed from sin.

"It was so quiet, then," Mrs. Bauer was saying. "After the blasphemies stopped. I held Billy in my arms, and his face looked so peaceful, and I knew that my son was saved at last. I told him it was time to go home, but he wouldn't move. He just lay there. I guess . . . I guess that means . . ."

She seemed to consider the question, but casually, as if it

were too remote to engage her. She turned her eyes on me again, and under their gaze I felt what Billy might have felt—what might have been his ultimate terror—that he wasn't real to her; that he was only a nuisance or a theorem or a thing, that there was nothing inside those eyes that would save him, no fellow feeling to put limits on what she might do.

She was like some being from another world, made of different stuff, who had never understood what it was to be human, who knew the word "love" but not the feeling, had never really known the feeling, though having been in human form.

$\triangledown$

Chapter 24

I COULD SEE BAUER just ahead, in the twilight, sitting on a log at the edge of the inlet. He was hunched over, as if in prayer, but his eyes were open. He was staring into the waters where Billy had died.

I stepped forward slowly, hoping I could get close to him before he noticed me. But something snapped beneath my shoe, and he looked up. When he saw who it was, he glared.

"Go away, Strickland. Leave me alone."

"I can't do that, Reverend."

"Yes, you can."

He reached down and lifted up a handgun. I stopped, sucking in my breath. My eyes measured the distance between us. He was about forty feet away, and a little below, down a small bank.

"Come on, Bauer, you don't want to do that."

"It's exactly what I want to do."

Bauer twisted his hand back, awkwardly, to point the gun at his chest. Then he shifted its position, putting his thumbs on the trigger, his fingers on the gun butt, the butt on his knee. While he made the shift, he watched me like an animal watching its natural enemy.

"Go easy," I said. "I'm staying right here."

After a moment he seemed to relax a little.

"What about Martha?" he asked. "Did you call the police?"

"I had to."

"Yes."

"They'll put her in a hospital where she'll get psychiatric evaluation. But, whatever they decide, you know she'll be in their hands for a long, long time."

"Yes." Bauer's eyes were sad, but his nod seemed resigned, maybe even a little relieved, as if some obligation had been lifted from him. He looked off toward the trees. "I hope what's left of life won't be too bad for her."

He was saying good-bye to her, to everything. He seemed bone-weary, as if the sadness in his eyes were a terminal disease metastasizing throughout his entire body. I knew I had to keep him talking, keep him distracted. If he gave himself up to that sadness, it would destroy him.

"Reverend, what do you say we just stop this nonsense and go on back. You've got some people worried sick about you. Think how happy they'd be to see that you're all right."

"How'd you find me?" he asked, ignoring what I'd said.

I shrugged. "As soon as I thought about it, I knew you'd be here."

"Because of Billy."

"And because of what I saw in your face back there. And because of what you told me about that river bank long ago. Still, I kept hoping you wouldn't have the gun."

"So much for hope."

"Is it the same gun?"

He took the heft of it, as if making sure. "I don't know why I kept it. Maybe to prove to myself that I had nothing to fear from it. Odd that after all this time I should end up right back where I started."

He looked down into the darkening water. Despair moved through the hollows and crevices of his face like a sea subsuming the land it had once shaped. His face must have had much the same look fourteen years ago when he'd raised that gun to his head. Only this time God didn't seem to be around to talk him out of it. Just me. And I wasn't sure I knew what to say.

"Reverend, this doesn't make any damned sense. It goes against everything you believe."

"Everything I used to believe."

"That's just shock talking."

"No." The word came out like a small cry. His chest rose and fell. "This is different, Strickland. Before, even in my worst moments, I could feel the Lord there. But I can't see His face anymore. All I can see is her face—the way she looked when she talked about killing Billy. God's light has gone out in me. I've never felt so cold in all my life."

"Bauer, it is shock. You're in no shape to judge what's happened. Give it time. You'll believe again."

"No. I won't."

"Then you'll believe something else. Everybody does."

"You don't."

"I believe you've got forever to be dead."

Bauer almost laughed. "That's a little bare for a philosophy, isn't it?"

"Maybe. But it's stupid of you to throw your life away like this. I know you're hurting like hell, and you just want the hurting to stop. You're furious, and you feel like destroying the world, and you can't, so you're going to destroy yourself. But if you'll just grit your teeth and hold on a little while, all that will change. The pain will get less. You'll even find some joy after a time."

"I don't care, Strickland. My son is gone, and I just don't care."

"Well, maybe you should care. What about all the people who care for you? You've got a whole congregation of them out there."

I thought I saw Bauer wince.

"And there's Elizabeth Tate," I said. "Do you have any idea how much in love with you she is?"

"I love her too." Bauer's eyes closed, leaking tears. His shoulders slumped, as if love were an unbearable weight.

I thought of trying to rush him, but the distance was too great, and with it the risk that I'd startle him into pulling the trigger. Instead I tried to maneuver a little closer, a step at a time, as in a children's game I dimly remembered. After a few steps I got caught, as his eyes opened.

"Don't come any closer, Strickland!" he screamed. "I mean it!"

There was fury in his eyes. He jabbed the gun barrel against his chest as if he were trying to stab himself with it.

"Okay, okay!" I took a step back. "Look, I've stopped."

His sudden show of violence had shaken me. Before, even though I'd known there was danger in his depression, the very passivity of it had given me false reassurance. Now I saw that he was really going to do it. A sick feeling went through me.

"Don't just stop," he said. "Go away. Don't you get it, Strickland? I've had all I'm going to take. I'm going to put this bullet in me, and there's nothing in the world you can do about it. If you try to rush me, I'll do it now. But I don't want that. And I don't want to spend my last few minutes arguing with you. I want a little time alone with Billy."

"Give me the gun," I said. "Then you can have all the time you want with Billy."

"No," he said. "I don't want to live. I just want to say good-bye."

"Bauer, that will change, you know it will, if you'll just give it time."

"I don't want to give it time." All his aggression had ebbed away, leaving exhaustion in its place. "Strickland, please. I've made up my mind. I don't want to live. I want to die. You can't stop me from doing this thing. Let me be. Give me these last few minutes alone. Please. As a friend."

The gentle despair in his pleading was so seductive, I would have given him almost anything. But not his death. Not here, now, in this kind of despair.

I just stood there. I couldn't bring myself to rush him, to make the movement that would almost certainly incite him to pull the trigger. But I couldn't bring myself to leave him either. I had a sudden vision of the two of us here forever, as in some medieval portrait of hell, argument and counter-argument, to no point, into eternity.

Perhaps Bauer sensed something like that as well. He gave a long, weary sigh. "Maybe it is too much to ask. I guess it's up to me. Here's what we're going to do. I'm going to count to ten. If you're not gone by then, Strickland, I'm going to pull the trigger. If you take so much as a step toward me, I'll pull it as soon as you do. I want you to go away and give me some time. If you want to force my hand by standing there or stepping toward me, that's up to you."

"Bauer . . ."

"One."

"Bauer, for Christ sake, wait a second now."

"Two."

"*Think*, God damn it. Will you just think about what you're . . ."

"Three."

"What about the people who love you? How do you think they'll feel when . . . ?"

"Four. I'm through listening to you, Strickland. I'm through arguing. Just go away. *Five.*"

The whole world seemed to drop suddenly, like a dip on an infinite roller coaster. It was hard to breathe. There was a ringing in the air all around me. The power seemed to go out of my limbs, making it difficult to stand.

"Six."

Turn and go, I told myself. At least then you won't be responsible. You won't have to watch. It'll buy some time, and maybe he'll change his mind after all.

But I couldn't move.

"Seven."

My vision darkened, and clouded, taking on the texture of a dream. I could still see Bauer there, pointing the gun at his chest. But he kept changing into another Bauer, his chest blown open, blood everywhere. There was so much blood.

"Eight."

The air all around me seemed to be churning, as if a storm were coming. I can't take this again, I kept thinking. Don't do this to me, you son of a bitch.

"Nine."

"You bastard!"

I realized with horror that I had taken a step toward Bauer, was now in fact striding toward him, screaming at him, blubbering like a child. But I saw all this as if from a great distance, powerless to stop it.

"You selfish son of a bitch! Go ahead. Blow your fucking head off. See if I care. I don't give a fuck anymore, you prick!"

I knew this had all gone wrong, horribly, ludicrously wrong, but the knowledge had absolutely no effect on what I was doing. Some part of me noticed in passing that Bauer was staring at me with his mouth hanging open.

"Strickland . . . ?"

"Go ahead, you shithead!" I yelled, still sobbing. "Why should you give a fuck about anyone else? Shoot, God damn you! Why in hell don't you shoot?"

I kept striding toward Bauer, weeping and screaming. I must have been a sight, judging from the expression on Bauer's face. He seemed totally bewildered, as he got to his feet, his body turned toward me, his gun hand dropping to his side.

"Strickland, what's wro—?" he started to ask.

Then withdrew the question, as my body came hurtling toward him.

I have no memory of leaping. I don't know if it was an impulse of madness or sense. Suddenly there I was, in mid-air, the hysteria gone, panic in its place, a voice inside me screaming the same thing over and over.

The gun, the gun, the gun.

Bauer was reacting now, but surprise and elevation had given me the advantage. He managed only half a step back, and half a gesture of defense, before my body hit his, my chest against his face, toppling us. We seemed to fall in slow motion, my hands crawling over his half-raised right arm toward his gun hand. I got it, but then we hit the ground, and I felt the gun go tumbling away.

After a dazed moment, I began feeling the ground for the gun, while I tried to squirm off Bauer, to extend my reach.

My fingertips touched metal, but Bauer's hand clamped on my hand, pulling my fingers away. He yanked my body back on top of his, then began twisting his body, trying to throw me off the other side. I grabbed at him, to keep him from the gun, and suddenly we were tumbling down the slope of the shore, splashing into the lake.

We ended up in shallow water, on our sides, face-to-face, pushing, pulling, jabbing, clutching, each trying to get free while keeping the other from getting free. I could feel in Bauer the greater strength, and the greater fury, and knew he'd get the best of me like this. When I felt him land an elbow, I let myself go limp, letting go, letting him start to get up. Then I kicked out, kicking him over and away.

We got to our feet at the same moment, a yard and a half apart, with me between him and the shore. He came at me, but he was in deeper water, his footing more precarious. I feigned a jab, then a shove, forcing him to shift his balance. When I saw him teeter, I turned and splashed toward shore. A second later I heard his splashing strides behind me—he hadn't fallen—but that second gained was all I needed. I made it to shore, grabbed the gun, then scrambled up the bank. At the top I began firing into the air, hearing from Bauer an anguished, "No, Strickland, no."

As I fired upward, I turned, and saw Bauer charging toward me. I heard the fourth shot, and the fifth, and the click of an empty chamber, then hurled the gun up and over the onrushing man. I was watching it sail toward the lake when Bauer hit me in the mouth.

I went down hard, felt Bauer jump on top of me, his fists flailing. I tried to get my arms over my face, tried to roll away, finally got Bauer in a clinch, pressing my face into the shelter of his shoulder. We kept struggling there on the ground, Bauer screaming, "God damn you, Strickland, God damn you," while his fists beat against my back, then crying, "Billy, Billy," as his fists stopped their beating, then giving out great wrenching sobs, as I just sort of held him.

Exhaustion ended it finally, and we rolled apart, on our backs, in the dust, gasping for air. I tried to be ready to move again, if he did, though I wasn't at all sure I could. Fortunately, he just lay still.

"Bauer," I said, when I could breathe again. "Are you all right?"

There was no answer. I turned my head toward him. His chest rose and fell with steady breathing. His eyes were open. He looked all right. Just angry. I turned back.

"It won't do any good to ignore me," I said. "You can't get rid of me. I don't care how many more days like this it takes. I'm not going to let you die."

"Why do you have to keep saving me?" said Bauer, plaintively. "Why can't you just leave me alone?"

"I can't, that's all. I won't."

Bauer gave a sigh, full of weariness. "I can't fight you, Strickland. I don't have another day like this left in me. I guess you win."

"Maybe we both do."

"Just don't expect me to thank you," he said, bitterly. "Don't ever expect that."

We continued to lie there, both of us too tired to move. Gradually I became aware that my mind was taking an inventory of injuries: a loose tooth, a wrenched knee, some ribs that made funny sounds when I breathed, the cuts and scapes visible through rips in my clothing. Right now I was under the anesthetic of fatigue. Later on I was going to hurt.

"Strickland."

"What?" I said, a bit sharply. Thinking about my injuries was making me irritable.

"I've got to know. Was that all a trick back there? The way you started screaming at me."

"No. No trick. I just kind of . . . lost it. I must have looked pretty funny, huh?"

"What happened?"

"I don't know," I said, as a reflex. "Yes, I do. I guess I'm just sick and tired of people dying on me. Sick and tired of people I care about giving up."

The ache in my voice surprised me. And the hint of tears I had to blink back. I guess some pains are harder to anesthetize.

I closed my eyes for a time. When I opened them again I saw that Bauer was propped up on one elbow, staring at me.

"It doesn't ever go away, does it?" he said. "That kind of pain."

I shook my head, feeling the gravel beneath it. "No. But it gets better."

"How much better?"

"I don't know. Why don't we both hang around for a while and find out."

Bauer nodded, but abstractedly, and I wasn't quite sure at what. He looked down at the ground. He began picking at small pieces of stone like someone tidying up.

"Strickland, I'm sorry for what I put you through today," he said. "You're a good person. I know you did what you thought was right. If I don't feel real grateful just now . . . well, maybe someday I will."

Bauer looked off toward the inlet and after a moment his eyes began to glaze over with sad reverie. I was about to say something to distract him, when a better distraction came: sounds of movement in the woods, and human voices.

I rose up on my elbows to look. People were coming out of the woods on the other side of the small inlet.

"Your friends," I said.

But Bauer's focus was more specific than mine. "Elizabeth," he whispered, and the life that came into his face at that moment gave me more hope for him than had all his weary concessions.

Bauer and I must have been a sight, lying there in the dirt, cut up, our clothing torn, soaked, and covered with mud and dust. Frantic questions were shouted all at once from the other side of the water. Bauer had no hope of answering them; he just kept yelling that we were all right.

I saw Elizabeth detach herself from the others and rush along the edge of the inlet to circle around to us. At the same moment, Bauer began struggling to his feet, giving out a couple of groans. Once up, he took a step toward Elizabeth, then seemed to remember himself. He stopped and leaned over, offering me his hand.

"Go on," I said, waving his hand away. "Go see her. I'll be along in a minute."

"You sure?"

"Yes. Just go. She's probably crazy with worry. Anyway, I could use a break. Maybe she can take care of you for a change."

Bauer actually smiled. "Maybe she can at that," he said, and then he was off.

I watched Bauer and Elizabeth come together in a tender fumbling of touch and reassurance, then the others reach Bauer, hugging or patting him, talking with him or at him, all with obvious relief and caring. A lot of people loved that man.

As I lay there, I began to feel my eyes and mind drawn toward dark waters and those in them. But I kept watching Bauer. There would be all the time in the world for those who were lost. Today was a day for one who was saved.